HUNTED PACK

SHELLEY MUNRO

MUNRO PRESS

Hunted Pack

Ebook ISBN: 978-1-99-106362-5
Print ISBN: 978-1-99-106363-2

Editor: Evil Eye Editing
Cover: Kim Killion, The Killion Group, Inc.

Munro Press, New Zealand.

First Munro Press electronic publication September 2024

First Munro Press print publication September 2024

DEDICATION

For Paul, my husband, partner in crime, and fellow
adventurer.
Every day is a good day.

INTRODUCTION

Small-town secrets often wriggle free...

Her New Year fling vanished without saying goodbye.

Learning that he's the new town cop shocks Claire, and unfortunately, tender feelings have blossomed. Crushing them is almost impossible, and strong, sexy Fergus wants nothing more than a casual friendship.

Shifter Fergus Murray hides his dragon status and upholds the human law in small-town Te Anau. A woman shattered his heart, and now he fiercely protects the remnants. Friends, he can do, but nothing more. Until Claire...

A werewolf's murder brings danger to town, and that's the start of the mysterious crimes and his humongous problems, especially when Claire gets dragged into the middle of the trouble.

Hunted Pack features a shapeshifter cop hunting for a murderer, a town full of secrets and gossip, and a human woman who can't deny her attraction to a paranormal man. She wants more than one night and is willing to give him a second chance to readjust his mindset. Friends to lovers is the ultimate destination.

Prologue

Fergus was halfway to drunk.

Around him, Queenstown locals and tourists shouted and laughed, hips wriggling to the rockin' music of the cover band. Groups of women in itty-bitty dresses flirted and tossed their hair while packs of young men eyed them with fervent interest. Lust seethed in the air along with the beat of the drums. The party had amped up during the last hour, the carefree mood a living, vibrant thing as the pub customers celebrated the creep toward the new year.

Only a few hours to go now.

He hadn't wanted to socialize, but he'd tagged along with a group of mates, not wanting to draw attention by staying at the hotel.

Fergus stared at the double whisky sitting on the bar in front of him—expensive Scottish malt, his heart heavy as he lifted the glass to his mouth. The woody scent hit him first, and he forced himself to go slow, to savor the smoky vanilla flavor instead of tipping the entire contents down his throat.

The sad truth? Even if he was getting a decent buzz, his non-human status meant he needed to keep up the rapid pace to dull his senses. He couldn't afford that—not on a junior cop's wages.

A failure.

On all levels.

Miranda's sneering words ripped through his mind, cutting through the drunken fuzziness and slashing at his heart again. *And again.*

She didn't want him.

His dragon status had scared her.

He'd thought... Hell, he didn't know what he'd thought.

But he'd never hurt her. He'd thought she'd understood. He was the same man he'd been before she'd known he was a dragon. The man who wanted to uphold the human law and keep citizens safe. It was all he'd ever wanted since an abusive uncle had murdered his best friend. From that moment, he'd wanted to be a cop. *The good guy.* But no matter how often he tried to explain, Miranda didn't get it.

"Excuse me, can I squeeze in beside you?"

Fergus blinked at the curvy woman, attempting to get the barman's attention. He was occupied at the far end of the bar while the woman serving closest to them focused on flirting with a burly wolf.

"Please." Her expression in her bright blue eyes echoed the warmth in her voice.

Unlike some women around him, she wasn't using coquettishness or flashing her tits to get what she wanted. Fergus's gaze dropped without conscious permission and lifted again to catch the firming of her mouth. Her confidence remained, but the friendliness he'd noted took a back seat to the glare she leveled at him.

Shame filtered into Fergus, and the gentlemanly manners his mother had drummed into him came to the fore. "Sorry."

He inched to the left to give her a slight gap. Fergus signaled to the closest bartender.

"What can I get you, handsome?" The slender redhead had flirted with him earlier, but he hadn't reciprocated. Not when her hair—the color and the style—reminded him of Miranda.

"The lady would like a drink."

The redhead's mouth firmed, but she pulled up professionalism and focused on the curvy woman who'd squeezed close.

Fergus froze, suddenly hyperaware of the woman's warmth against his arm and the subtle scent of vanilla and cedarwood drifting from her. A touch of sweetness with earthiness for balance.

"I'll have a bottle of bubbly," the woman said, pointing to the assortment of bottles in the bar fridge. "The brut one, please."

Her melodic voice pleased his dragon, his animalistic half drawing forward in curiosity. This close, the freckles on her cheeks and across the bridge of her nose stood out, and he smiled, charmed. She was attractive, that sleek

5

curtain of black hair making his fingers itch to touch.

"I'll pay for that," Fergus said.

"Oh, you don't have to do that," she said, smiling.

"Please, I'd like to. No expectations on my part, I promise." He meant it, too. Miranda had not only rejected him but, a week later, married a billionaire who lived in Auckland. She hadn't wasted time after she'd packed up and left the flat they'd shared in Dunedin.

"Thank you," she said finally after staring at him for a long, gut-twisting moment. "My name is Claire."

"Fergus," he said, rising. "Take my barstool."

"No, I'm here with a girlfriend. She's saving me a seat..." She glanced over her shoulder and trailed off. "Perhaps not," she muttered under her breath. "Thank you. If you're sure you don't mind."

Fergus followed her gaze to where a blonde woman slow-danced with a dark-haired man dressed in a suit. He couldn't see the man's face, but the woman's expression screamed love.

"Your friend?"

"Yeah, I thought they'd split. It was why she asked me to come out with her tonight. She wanted to party but not alone," Claire said.

"I came with friends," Fergus said. "They're around somewhere." Possibly they'd ditched him since at least one had accused him of dragging down the mood.

They had several more drinks, taking turns paying. They discussed everything from how expensive it was to live in or visit Queenstown to hiking and the various adrenaline sports available in the area. They people-watched and made up silly stories about their fellow revelers, and Fergus was glad. He didn't want to discuss anything profound or give personal details.

"Everyone seems determined to partner up tonight," Claire said, watching the couples on the dance floor.

Fergus understood. No one wanted to feel alone when everyone else was celebrating.

The singer held the final note of a frantic dance tune, and the crowd cheered. He grinned. "The final song before our new year countdown. Grab your partner and celebrate life."

"Would you like to dance?" Fergus asked.

"We'll lose our seat," Claire said.

"I'm going after the countdown."

"Oh," Claire said.

Had that been disappointment? Fergus wasn't sure and didn't trust his instincts right now. Miranda had fooled him good, making him doubt his judgment.

"Claire!"

Claire's friend stood behind them, her hand clasped in Suitman's. "Jerry and I are leaving now. Will you be okay?"

"Sure," Claire said. "The hotel isn't far to walk. It should be safe enough."

"I'm staying with Jerry," the woman said.

"Thanks for letting me know. Happy New Year!"

Claire was pissed. Fergus wasn't sure how he knew because her smile remained intact. Friendly. Her friend didn't notice, and the guy she was with—Jerry—wasn't interested in anyone or anything.

The woman gave Claire a brief hug before leaving

without a backward glance.

"You don't like Jerry," Fergus said.

"He's arrogant and has a temper. They've known each other since childhood, and their parents want the match. It's not up to me to butt in and express my doubts to Laura."

The singer crooned about kids in love, and Fergus reached for Claire's hand. "Let's dance."

Claire slid her hands under Fergus's shirt and smoothed her palms over his warm back. Fergus's soft lips caressed her neck, and her heart rate kicked into a racy beat. She'd never done anything like this, yet that didn't stop her from sliding the shirt she'd unbuttoned off his broad shoulders because she instinctively trusted this somber man with sad brown eyes.

"Claire?"

"Kiss me," she breathed.

Fergus didn't hesitate. He drew her close, and the rising passion easily surpassed their first kiss—the one they'd shared on the dance floor as the clock struck midnight.

Things had moved swiftly after that, and she found herself alone with him in her hotel room, her little black dress on the floor, and her wearing just her lacy black underwear and strappy black shoes.

Fergus's pale blue shirt fluttered to the carpet, and as they continued to kiss, it became a competition to see who could get naked first.

He parted their lips, and they were both breathing hard. "Are you sure?"

"Yes," she said. She might have doubts tomorrow, but what did it matter? She was leaving town and returning to her new home of Te Anau. Her parents had left her a holiday cottage there, and she'd bought a pub. Living the dream.

Why not start her year with a bang?

Claire stifled her giggle. She had a happy buzz but wasn't drunk. Yes, she'd grab the fleeting pleasure now because once she returned to Te Anau, she'd be too busy for personal shenanigans. All work and no play.

Fergus pulled back a fraction as if to reassure himself of her consent.

She sank onto the edge of the king-size bed and lifted her right foot, waggling it at him. "Help me off with my shoes?"

He did without hesitation, his warm hands cradling her foot and pressing into the arch once he'd slipped off the black sandal. He repeated his actions with her left foot before lifting her easily and tossing her into the middle of the mattress.

"Hmm," she said. "I love your dragon tattoo. It's amazing." The black dragon covered most of his back, its tail curving around his hip.

"Thanks."

Seconds later, his muscular body held her captive. He surrounded her, and when she should've experienced fear, she encountered excitement instead. He kissed and caressed, taking his time to explore her body with his work-roughened hands. Her bra came free with a simple twist of his wrist.

Claire took a moment to wonder before pushing her questions aside. One night. Joy and pleasure. No interrogations.

His hot mouth closed around her nipple, and she sighed, enjoying the suction and the abrasion of his jaw against her flesh. A moan slipped free, and she couldn't find it in herself to feel embarrassment.

He chuckled and continued teasing her flesh. The pleasuring stroke of his fingers across her other nipple had her gasping, her steady rise to arousal making her restless and needy.

"Shush," he whispered. "Let me make you feel good."

His tongue ran across the swell of her stomach as he repositioned himself. He drew her panties downward, and she lifted her hips in silent aid. Fergus tossed the filmy black material away and turned back to her, his eyes a golden brown and full of sultry promise.

"Close your eyes and concentrate on what you're feeling," he whispered.

Her heart thundered as she obeyed. Shutting down one of her senses made the others strain to gain information.

"So pretty," he whispered, his voice thick and much deeper.

Before she could reply, the stroke of his fingers had desire kicking her in the belly. She wanted this so much. Wanted him.

Claire moved her hips in silent demand, lifting into his light touch. Her legs fell open in blatant disregard for modesty. Cool air whispered across her heated flesh before she felt the softness of his tongue. The firm sweep across her clit had her groaning and a plea settling on her lips. She bit it back, gasping instead as his fingers came into play, teasing and arousing her. A shudder ran through her as he played her body like a pro.

He sucked and tasted. Explored and surrounded her aching nub with his lips. The light suction slammed passion to life, and when he coupled this with his fingers, sliding one digit into her warm heat and stroking her internally, she exploded. The spasms tore through her, and her sex clenched around his finger.

Gradually, she came down, her pulse slowing.

He rose up the bed and kissed her, slow and deep. It was brief, way too fast. Embarrassingly quick.

"Let me grab a condom," he murmured.

Her eyes flew open, and she saw to her consternation that he still wore his trousers. He grabbed his wallet and pulled out a condom. The fabric of his pants rustled as he dropped them and his underwear. Then he stalked toward the bed, not shy about his nakedness.

She had a glimpse of trim hips, his erection, and part of his sexy tattoo that curled around his hip and one shoulder. Fergus turned off the light before she heard the crinkle of the condom wrapper.

Soon he was on the bed and kissing her again.

She'd thought he'd be in a hurry, but he seemed to take pleasure from caressing and kissing her breasts and any other body part within reach. By the time he entered her, stretching her flesh with his girth, she was almost desperate with need again.

She'd picked the perfect man for a one-night fling.

His expertise and generosity would ruin her for other men.

He pushed deep, filling her in a most delightful manner before slowly withdrawing and thrusting home again. Desire flared in her, the tiny tremors of her flesh grasping his cock. She gripped his shoulders, giving into her desire to kiss and touch his splendid body. It surpassed her wildest carnal fantasies.

"Are you close?" he whispered.

"Yes."

Fergus changed the tempo of his strokes, going faster and thrusting deep while holding her protectively. This time wasn't as quick, but it was no less memorable. She arched into his strokes, falling into bliss. He rocked into her, keeping his moves slow before his breath caught. His next push was fast, flesh slapping against flesh as he strove for completion.

He groaned, released a pent-up breath as he thrust home, then held still. A long moment later, he twisted their bodies so Claire lay partially on top of him.

"That was amazing," he said. "Thank you."

"It was fantastic on my end, too," Claire said.

He held her for a few minutes before moving. "Let me dispose of the condom before we cuddle a bit and get some sleep."

"Okay." *Be still my beating heart.* The man intended to cuddle her.

He was back quickly, placing something on the bedside

cabinet.

"Another condom for later," he said.

Worked for her.

He woke her at some stage. She couldn't have guessed at the time and didn't ask. But the sex was stupendous, and she wasn't about to waste time with stupid questions.

When she woke again, daylight pierced her hotel room. She rolled over and found the bed empty; the only evidence of his presence was the lingering soreness in her limbs and the head impression on the pillow.

"Fergus?" Claire sat upright, but she was alone.

Fergus had left without saying goodbye.

Four months later.

Throughout the day, the locals gossiped about the new cop who'd arrived to replace their community constable. Constable Davies had retired after a health scare, saying he wanted to spend more time fishing.

"He's gorgeous and single," one of her regulars said. She was a solo mum who'd had a rough time after her husband had run off with the owner of the funeral home.

"Have you seen him?" another single woman asked.

"Yep, I want his boots beneath my bed," a third woman said, a determined glint in her eyes. She fanned her face with her hand. "Hawt stuff!"

If Claire had a chance, she'd warn the poor guy. No man deserved this high level of scrutiny, and the last thing they wanted was to scare him off. Te Anau desperately needed a community constable.

"He's tall. It's difficult to tell, but I'd bet my next paycheck the man has stacks of muscles under his uniform shirt." The woman, barely out of her teens, cocked her head, making her blonde ponytail tip to the side. "His eyes are brown and soulful."

Claire barely restrained her snort at that gem, but she wiped across the bar, clearing away water splashes and eavesdropping on the small-town gossip.

Another woman continued the description. "He has brown hair with blond highlights that look natural. When I saw him, he was at the school crossing, speaking with the kids walking to school. He has a lovely smile."

Claire didn't hear anymore since the local stock agent strode up to the bar, his expression harried and his dark hair sticking up as if he'd dragged his fingers through it several times. "Something wrong, Kerry?" she asked.

"One of the trucks has broken down. It has a full load of my heifers destined for sale. The driver will be late, and I'm gonna miss my slot. I'd love a rum, but I'd better settle for a flat white," he said.

"Sure thing," Claire said, pushing a button to grind the coffee beans.

"Have you met the new cop?" he asked.

"No, but everyone is talking about him. So far, opinion is favorable."

Kerry nodded, showing his agreement with her assessment. "I spoke to him a few minutes ago when I reported a dozen loose sheep on the road. He's young but not arrogant. I liked him." Kerry lowered his voice. "He'll be popular with the ladies since he's single. Easy on the eye, according to my wife."

Claire had already gathered that from her eavesdropping. Her mind drifted to Fergus, the man she'd met in Queenstown. He'd been tall with brown eyes. She sighed and focused on heating the milk for the coffee. Kerry hated too much froth.

She handed over the takeaway coffee cup and accepted a ten-dollar note. After ringing up the order, she gave Kerry his change.

"I told the constable you make excellent coffee and food here," Kerry said.

"Thanks for the recommendation," Claire said. "I hope the truck issue gets resolved fast."

"Me, too," Kerry said.

Claire made coffee for an Australian couple and sold a sandwich to a Canadian girl who told her she'd arrived in Te Anau yesterday and was walking the Kepler track starting tomorrow.

Between customers, Claire answered a phone query about accommodation for the following week and refilled the beer fridge. She sliced a lemon for garnishing drinks.

A lull in the conversation had her lifting her head. A man had entered the bar, tall and wearing a cop's uniform. As he stalked closer, her gaze lifted to his face, and she froze. A sharp pain in her finger had her cursing and dropping the knife. She grabbed a paper towel before she bled all over the lemon slices.

"Fergus," she whispered.

His steps slowed—a sort of stutter in the fluidness of

his stride—before he recovered. "Claire. I didn't know you lived in Te Anau."

The statement came close to an accusation, and she scowled.

One of the women from the singles group appeared at the bar beside Fergus. "Do you know Constable Murray?"

"We've met once," Fergus said, his words decisive with an edge of warning directed at her.

Claire winced. She'd thought about this man ever since their one night in Queenstown. Dreamed and fantasized about him. Every other man had paled beside him, but it was obvious from his abrupt speech that he wanted nothing to do with her.

"How can I help you?" Claire said, amazed she could keep her voice so steady.

"A tea with milk, please," he said. "I also wanted to have a word about underage drinking."

"I don't sell alcohol to underage people. Or inebriated people," she added for good measure.

"Can I get you something, Natalie?" Claire asked the woman hovering beside Fergus.

"I wanted to invite the constable for dinner." She flashed him a winsome smile. "Save you looking through your unpacked boxes for pots and pans."

Claire held her tongue with difficulty. It was best to let the new cop speak for himself.

"Thank you, but I've unpacked my kitchen and filled my fridge. That was the first thing I did."

"But who will cook for you?" Natalie asked.

"My mother taught me to cook." He smiled at Natalie,

a smile that was way too friendly for Claire's liking.

Claire wanted to jump between the pair and tell Natalie to back off. She didn't move a muscle. Fergus had made his position clear. She should suck it up and avoid making a spectacle of herself.

"Besides my busy work schedule, I'm dealing with the aftermath of a broken relationship. I won't be scintillating company." Fergus turned to her. "Claire, my tea, please."

Heat suffused her cheeks as she turned away. Natalie said something to Fergus, but she barely heard his rumbly reply since the hot water pouring into the cup was loud. She made the tea, and when she turned back, Fergus was alone.

"It's nice to see you again, Claire. A familiar face to explain local things will be helpful. A friend."

His intense brown gaze turned golden for an instant. She gulped, another surge of heat flooding her cheeks. "Friends with benefits," she blurted.

No sooner had the words emerged than she wanted to haul them back.

Fergus blinked before he shook his head, set a ten-dollar note down, picked up his tea, and stepped back from the bar. "Friends without benefits."

The silence between them lengthened, and Claire wanted to melt into the floor, so acute was her embarrassment. "Of course," she managed in a strangled voice, her words scarcely louder than her thumping heart.

"Friends," he said firmly and strode away without waiting for his change.

1

FLIES BUZZED—THE ANGRY DRONE of dozens of insects in a food frenzy. A shift in the wind brought a ghastly metallic stench. Although the sun beat overhead, hotter than average for an October morning, a shiver ran through Constable Fergus Murray.

"Samuel?" he called, caution filling his voice.

When his friend didn't answer, Fergus halted halfway up the driveway. His nostrils flared as he pulled his dragon senses closer to the surface.

The sweetness of flowers rode the air, along with a faintly gamey scent he couldn't identify. He stepped off the gravel driveway onto the vibrant green lawn that needed mowing again because spring rains had swept through last week. Typical New Zealand weather for this time of the year. The pungent aroma and the buzz of insects increased as Fergus neared the brown gate on the right side of his white bungalow.

With his senses screaming, Fergus took a cautious step into the garden. His fingers tightened on the bag of sandwiches he'd purchased from his favorite bakery and the plastic container holding the chocolate cake Melissa Jacobson had dropped at the station. While he didn't want a romantic relationship, he wasn't about to turn down cake or the other goodies the single and married ladies brought him. *Since he was a bachelor, living on his own,* they invariably said.

A blowfly struck his face, and he flapped it away with an impatient hand.

"Samuel?" he called again, his gut churning. Something was off. *Wrong.* He set the container and sandwich bag on the front deck and focused on his screaming inner alarm.

Under most circumstances, he'd charge in and let his size and dragon power take control of whatever situation faced him. Not with Samuel, though. An ex-soldier and a werewolf, Samuel didn't take well to surprises.

It had taken Fergus months to gain Samuel's trust and persuade him to move into the tiny cottage at the rear of Fergus's home.

"Samuel?"

When he received no reply, Fergus followed his nose. He strode past a shrub with red flowers and came to an abrupt halt, a curse spewing from him on spotting a wolf lying by the vegetable patch. Blood matted its gray fur and pooled beneath the still body. Flies buzzed and landed, feasting on the gore.

Fergus crossed the distance in seconds to squat beside the still body. He cupped his hand over the wolf's nostrils.

Not breathing. He placed his fingers against the wolf's chest and noted the body was still warm.

With a heavy heart, he stood to observe the scene with a dispassionate eye. He buried his emotions, his distress at losing a friend, and stepped into his cop shoes. No footprints marked the ground apart from the ones within the vegetable patch. The tread mark and size matched the worn gray runners near the body. An old red T-shirt lay near the shoe, almost faded to pink. It looked as if someone had ripped the garment down the middle. A pair of well-worn jeans had suffered similar treatment. Fergus suspected Samuel's shift had burst through him before he could disrobe.

But why?

Much like Fergus, Samuel kept mainly to his two-legged form. Despite their pretty, politically correct words, Samuel hadn't trusted the humans to keep their word and afford shifters equal footing. Although he'd remained tight-lipped about his military stint, Fergus assumed the roots of Samuel's wariness had been sown during his service.

And now, someone had murdered him.

Fergus studied the scene, noting every detail. He snapped pictures of Samuel's wolf, his torn clothes, and discarded shoes. His nostrils flared wide as he breathed deeply to analyze the air. That wild, gamey scent again. It wasn't Samuel's wolf but something else Fergus had never encountered.

He'd spotted Samuel earlier this morning coming back from a run. That had been around six. Fergus had headed to the station shortly afterward, and they'd exchanged a wave. What had happened during the intervening time? Samuel hadn't mentioned problems, not that he would. Fergus usually heard of concerns via local gossip. Small towns. Nine times out of ten, keeping an ear on rumors allowed him to head off problems in his district before they occurred.

Fergus swallowed hard before quashing his churning emotions. He couldn't help Samuel if he allowed sorrow to govern his actions. What he needed was a calm mindset, and he'd require assistance from the Invercargill police.

He did another careful circuit of the body, but apart from the strange aroma, there was nothing to point Fergus in the culprit's direction. He collected his food before striding inside and leaving it in the kitchen. After a second of thought, he pulled a freshly laundered sheet from the hot water cupboard. On his return, Fergus swatted at the flies and carefully covered Samuel. Then, with a loud sigh, he dialed his superior officer.

"Sergeant Jackson," a brisk masculine voice barked.

"It's Constable Fergus Murray at Te Anau. I have a paranormal murder."

A lengthy pause ensued before a harsh grunt rippled down the line. "Are you certain?"

"Yes," Fergus said simply.

Another grunt. "Hell," Jackson said in disgust. "We had to have the first one. How do you know it's a paranormal creature? What is it?"

Fergus bit back his instinctive retort. While different paranormal species had come out in many countries, the

New Zealand government had been the first to give them equal legal status to humans. The small country's ballsy move garnered global attention, but experts were now urging for more public consultation. The government hadn't listened because many of them were paranormals themselves. To Fergus's surprise, there had been little trouble, and New Zealanders were getting on with their lives after the decimating effects of COVID-19 only eight years prior.

"Are you there?" Jackson barked.

"The murder victim is a werewolf. It looks as if someone thumped him over the head and stabbed him. I know he's a werewolf because he's my gardener/handyman."

"But you didn't see the murder occur?"

Fergus hesitated. He'd kept his dragon identity secret since he'd noted the attitudes of his bosses and the other cops he had dealings with during his duties. In a split-second decision, he said, "No. I arrived home and found the wolf's body in my garden. My handyman's clothes are nearby, and judging by the rips in the fabric, he did a rapid shift."

"I see," Sergeant Jackson said, and Fergus straightened at the man's tone. The pause lengthened, and Fergus thanked the stars he wasn't standing in his boss's office because the urge to shuffle his feet ate at him.

"I've taken scene photos," Fergus said. "Where should I send the body for an autopsy? Is it possible to assign another officer to the investigation?"

Still, his boss remained silent. Fergus frowned. Had the call dropped off? Something that happened in Te Anau because of the mountainous region. "Are you there?"

"I'm here," Jackson snapped.

Fergus pulled a face.

"No," Jackson said finally. "I can't spare the personnel right now. We're having trouble with the local gangs."

Fergus's hand tightened on his phone, and he bit back his instinctive retort. "What should I do with the body?" He kept his voice even as anger flashed through him. Samuel deserved better than this, and he'd do his best to uncover the identity of the person who'd murdered his friend.

Sergeant Jackson sighed. "Seek advice from a local GP or vet. Let them assess the body. Document the cause of death, write a report, and email it to me. We must take action, especially if a human dies later."

"Of course, sir," Fergus said in a neutral voice, even as disgust flooded him. It sounded as if he was on his own to investigate this murder. Hell, he wasn't even sure if their local vet would examine Samuel's body.

Apart from Samuel, Fergus was the only other paranormal in the area, and they'd kept the information to themselves. He didn't know Samuel's reasons and hadn't asked. Fergus found it easier doing his job without side-eyes from other cops and management. He'd seen how they treated paranormal officers—skilled and experienced cops who'd deserved better. His goal was to do his best for humans and paranormals, which was impossible if the locals feared him.

"Right," Sergeant Jackson said. "I look forward to your report."

The loud click confirmed his superior had hung up, and Fergus cursed under his breath. This wasn't right. It made him glad he'd concealed his true identity. Many people, like Jackson, believed paranormals couldn't safely integrate or interact with humans. Bigoted people who hated non-humans and considered them inferior.

They feared what they didn't understand, yet the truth was paranormal creatures had lived among the human population for hundreds of years, with no one being wiser. He could annihilate the population if he wished, as could many others. They didn't because they enjoyed peaceful lives instead of this blatant discrimination.

Fergus slipped his phone into his pocket and walked another circuit of the body. Now that his initial shock had faded, he might spot something he'd missed during his first scrutinization of the area. Then, he'd visit the vet surgery in person to ask for help.

He wanted to witness Nikau Brown's expression when he requested aid. While he'd always liked the other man whenever he'd met him, this was too important to leave to chance. If Nikau showed the slightest sign of prejudice, he'd contact another vet from farther afield.

Fergus discovered one partial footprint that didn't look like his or Samuel's. He snapped a photo and jotted a note covering his impressions of what he saw, length and depth, the front zigzag tread that was visible to the naked eye. Once he'd done that, he combed the area for anything that struck him as unusual. He bagged and labeled Samuel's clothes and footwear.

"Nothing else out of the ordinary." Fergus crouched

beside Samuel's body, flicking a sheet corner dislodged by the breeze back into position. "Samuel, my friend, what happened to you? There's nothing here worth stealing, so why did someone kill you?"

When the wind continued to play with the sheet edges, Fergus pegged the cover in place with nails from his toolshed. He noted all his woodwork tools were in their usual positions, and nothing seemed disturbed. Samuel's gardening implements were all in position, clean and sparkling as Samuel had left them.

This murder baffled him, but everyone left traces behind, no matter how smart they were. Perhaps someone had noted a stranger entering his property, or one of his neighbors had heard something. As soon as he spoke to Nikau, he'd spread out his investigation.

Samuel had fought for this country and kept his werewolf identity a secret when many others embraced the new freedoms offered by the government. After he'd limited his alcohol intake, he'd become a model citizen, deserving of the second chance Fergus had given him.

With one last check of the sheet covering Samuel's body, Fergus left his garden. He locked the gate when he usually didn't bother.

Determined to save time, he jumped into his work vehicle instead of walking, as he often did. Five minutes later, he entered the vet surgery, strode to the counter, and asked the elderly receptionist to speak to Nikau Brown.

"Nikau is with a patient," the woman said. "Once he finishes, you're welcome to see him."

"How long will he be?"

"Perhaps five or ten minutes."

"I'll wait. Does Nikau have more appointments?"

"Nope," the blonde woman replied. "It's been quiet today."

As promised, Fergus didn't wait for long.

"Fergus," Nikau said, extending his hand in welcome. He was a tall man with the tawny brown skin and black hair of a Māori, while his pale blue eyes showed his partial European ancestry. His grin was all confident male, and he held himself with dignity. "I haven't seen you for a few weeks. What can I do for you today?"

Aware of the receptionist listening to their conversation, Fergus jerked his head toward Nikau's office.

Nikau took the hint. "Come and grab a seat in my office. Would you like a coffee? I'm going to have one."

"Sure, a black coffee would hit the spot," Fergus said and claimed a seat while Nikau busied himself, popping a capsule into a machine. Seconds later, the rich aroma of coffee flooded the office.

Nikau set a coffee in front of him and busied himself with making another.

On his return, he dropped into his chair with a heavy sigh. "I stayed up all night assisting a late-calving cow. The calf died, and I don't think the cow will make it either."

Fergus met Nikau's gaze, noting the redness of his eyes. "I'm sorry, but what I'm going to tell you isn't good news." Fergus peered at the vet, unsure how the man would react to his request. He puffed out a burst of air to steel himself. "You know Samuel, the homeless soldier?"

"Yes." Curiosity blazed in Nikau's eyes as he sipped his

coffee.

"Someone murdered him this morning."

"What?" Nikau's hand froze mid-air, his coffee sloshing over the rim of his cup before he leveled it. "Who? How? Why are you telling me?"

Fergus paused. Now came the tricky part. He'd learn if he could count on Nikau when word leaked out—as it would. This small, close-knit community harbored an efficient rumor mill.

Nikau cocked his head, his intelligence and curiosity apparent, and repeated, "Why me?"

"Samuel was a werewolf, and he died in his wolf form. I need your help to catch the murderer." Fergus held his breath and focused on Nikau without blinking, waiting for the slightest sign of distaste.

He didn't see any.

Instead, Nikau's gaze sharpened. "A werewolf? How do you think he died?"

"A stab wound. There's lots of blood."

"Why are you asking me, rather than the Invercargill police?"

"I've spoken to them. They're not coming." Fergus left his explanation at that.

"They're not coming because Samuel is a paranormal creature." Nikau's voice sounded flat. Disbelieving.

"Yes."

Nikau downed the last of his coffee and stood. "Many locals scorned Samuel. I didn't know he was a werewolf, but I'll help all I can."

"Thank you," Fergus said, rising too. His first hurdle

cleared. At least Nikau seemed to be open-minded. So far, Fergus and Samuel were the only *others* in Te Anau. Hell, even the human population had dwindled after the COVID pandemic when the country had closed to tourists. There were dozens of empty shops and business premises around the town.

"My sister is married to a taniwha. They live in South Auckland. Papakura. They're good men and women, and I'd trust them with my life," Nikau said. "They're living openly since the new laws, but that doesn't mean I don't hear about the problems they experience." He shook his head. "In the past, skin color mattered, but now it also depends on whether you're considered human or *other*. I won't discuss this with my friends, but I wanted you to understand why I'm offering my services. That you're requesting my help speaks highly of you."

Fergus grunted. "Thanks. I have my vehicle. What equipment do you require?"

Five minutes later, they were on the road, and Fergus breathed more freely. Samuel might've looked fierce and taken limited baths, but he'd been a decent man beneath his sullen prickliness. It hadn't been his fault the war in the Middle East had haunted him.

"This way," Fergus said once he and Nikau climbed from the police vehicle.

"You didn't say the murder occurred at your place."

"No," Fergus agreed.

"Any estimate about the time of murder?"

"Samuel stayed in the cottage at the rear of my house. He only agreed to stay there if I let him care for my outdoor space. Whoever killed him attacked while he was working in the garden. My best guess is that it occurred shortly after I left for work. One thing puzzles me, though. The number of flies around the body."

Nikau shot him a sidelong glance. "Flies? It's too cold for most insects here."

"I know. I covered Samuel with a sheet before I came to see you."

Fergus opened the gate and ushered Nikau into his garden. He cursed as the body came into view. The sheet was covered in a thick swarm of flies.

"I've never seen anything like this," Nikau murmured, his manner sorrowful and respectful. "The flies are a weird violet color in the light."

"I hadn't noticed that," Fergus said. "I'll unpeg the sheet and trap the flies at the same time."

"Have you taken photos? Can we move the body to my surgery?"

Fergus hesitated, but given the swarm of flies, which had grown larger while he'd been away, Nikau had a valid point. "Okay. Let's do this."

2

CLAIRE BRYCE SURVEYED THE lingering lunchtime patrons and frowned. Fergus usually checked in with the various businesses most days and nights. He'd begun visiting once the rush subsided. He was friendly and polite to everyone, and Claire *still* had a crush on him despite him telling her they'd be nothing but friends. Who wouldn't with his competent if silent manner and tall, muscular physique? Then there were his deep chocolate brown eyes that missed nothing and his brown sun-streaked hair.

She wasn't the only woman in Te Anau to fantasize about Fergus Murray. Since he'd arrived in the town almost seven months ago, she'd learned via gossip that he'd dated a Dunedin woman for two years before she'd up and moved to Auckland for her job. They'd been engaged, and everyone had expected them to announce their wedding date. No one was sure what had happened because Fergus wasn't talking. Those at Gossip Central had invented answers of their own. Claire heard the woman hated kids. She hadn't wanted marriage and that Fergus was lousy in bed. *Yeah, right.* Fergus radiated quiet confidence, and their one night together had shown her he was an exceptional lover who focused on his partner's pleasure.

A fly buzzed past her, the loud drone bringing a frown as she tracked its path. A blowfly. The last thing she needed—flies for the rare tourists to complain about.

She marched to her office to retrieve a can of fly spray and a bright red swatter. Upon her return, she found only three customers remaining. *Perfect.* Another quiet day with low takings. She sighed and pushed away her misgivings. Business would improve soon. *It would.*

Now, where was that fly? Ah! She stalked it with her swatter, preferring to kill it instantly rather than use the spray. It landed on a chair in a patch of sunlight. She inched closer, positioning herself to wield her weapon. Huh! The bothersome insect was a pretty violet color in the sunlight.

She struck with an audible slap against the wood.

The violet-black body dropped to the floor and didn't move again. Claire picked it up with a napkin and dropped it into the trash behind the bar. She stowed her swatter in the cleaning cupboard, washed her hands, and used her downtime to stock the bar fridges.

Immediately, her thoughts turned to Fergus. She was positive he liked her, and she sensed the weight of his stare whenever she was serving customers. The man didn't strike her as shy since he never had trouble speaking with the town's residents. The tough cop dealt with the locals, ranging from the cranky Mrs. Green, who drove her old

Holden like a tank, knocking over trash bins and scraping other vehicles, to the youngest child who'd skinned their knee at the local fair. No, shyness wasn't his problem. The man was private, and while she respected that about him, it was maddening. Frustrating.

She huffed out her vexation and wished this inconvenient crush would fade away.

Claire tsked, rotating a beer bottle until the label faced forward. To her chagrin, she wasn't the only woman interested in Fergus Murray. She'd thought it earlier, and the truth floated through her thoughts now. He showed no favoritism, and the more vocal of the women were speculating about his gender preference.

Claire would have to settle for the friendship he'd told her was on offer.

Liar!

She gave a self-deprecating chuckle and moved to the second fridge to fill the gaps in the soda cans.

"Private joke?" a masculine voice asked, a frisson of humor dancing in his words.

Claire jumped, jerked her head, and collided with the glass door. Flustered, she rose, heat flooding her face while she rubbed her ouchie. She turned to face the object of her thoughts—Constable Fergus Murray. Her eyes widened at his wan, exhausted appearance. "What's wrong? What's happened?"

He hesitated, his broad shoulders shifting a fraction. "Someone murdered Sam this morning."

"What?" Claire gripped the edge of the bar until the color fled her knuckles. "Who? Why? Samuel never hurt anyone."

"I don't know," Fergus said. "Can I have a tea, please?"

"Do you have any suspects? Should we be worried?"

Fergus ignored the questions, and she figured it was a testimony to his unease that she'd extracted any information from him. While she went to the coffee machine for boiling water and made Fergus his tea, he fired questions at her.

"When did you last see Samuel?"

"Yesterday, when he came in with you for dinner," Claire said with a glance over her shoulder.

"You didn't see him this morning during your run?"

Claire blinked. She'd only recently started running again, and it was barely light when she ran the Te Anau streets. She hadn't known Fergus knew of her exercise routine. Claire rolled her shoulders, shifting her weight from foot to foot, unable to meet his piercing brown eyes. Had he seen her red face and sweaty hair? The way she breathed like a steam train?

"Claire." Clear impatience rang in his voice, startling her because Fergus was always calm and even-tempered. Nothing rattled him, not even the group of predatory single women determined to break through his disinterest.

She set the tea on the bar for him and poured herself a glass of water before rounding the bar to sit beside him. "No, I saw the delivery truck at the supermarket, and three or maybe four cars passed me while I was jogging along the lakeside. I haven't seen Sam since last night. I can't believe... This is terrible."

Fergus's mouth firmed, but he didn't comment.

Instead, he picked up his teacup and took a sip.

"Have you eaten? I can heat something for you."

A shudder passed through Fergus. "No, I can't stomach the idea of eating right now. Nikau and I—" He broke off. "I'll eat later."

Claire stared at him through narrowed eyes. "Why was Nikau working with you? What about Doc Jones?"

Fergus straightened, his tone flat. "I won't answer that."

Before she could question Fergus further, two couples entered. The women seated themselves while the men ventured to the bar to check out beer options.

"Let's try a local beer," one man suggested. Sweat dotted his forehead, and he wiped it away with the back of his hand. His belly pressed against the bar as he attempted to see the available beers.

Claire stepped behind the bar and into her professional shoes. She pointed out the local beers and poured two testers for the men. Their accents told her they'd come from Australia.

"We'll take a pint of this one," the taller, sparer Australian said. "Our wives would like a glass of sauvignon blanc—a local one, if possible."

Claire recommended one from a Cromwell winery.

"Do you have food?"

Claire wasn't about to turn away tourist money despite the cook's absence. "The kitchen is closed, but I can do vegetable soup or steak pie with chips and salad. If you prefer a snack, we have garlic bread, or I could make a bowl of potato or kumara wedges with sour cream and sweet chili sauce."

Tall Man nodded. "We'll be back with our order in a few minutes."

"Can I have another tea, please, Claire?"

Fergus's baritone sent a shudder of awareness through her, and if it hadn't been for another customer entering, she might have done something stupid. Instead, she grasped his empty cup and retreated, thankful he didn't seem aware of her flustered state. By the time she'd made him another and added a chocolate chip cookie, the Australians had returned to order, and she had two customers waiting.

She took care of the meal orders first, poured a handle of lager, and then mixed a gin and tonic.

"Fergus, can you watch the bar and give me a shout if I get customers?" Takings were down this week, which wasn't ideal. She'd grab business while she could.

Fergus grunted, and she took that as permission. She'd fallen for a tall, mysterious guy with a quiet intensity that attracted every woman's eye, and they saw each other enough for her to call them friends of sorts. She'd fallen for him that first night, and he didn't seem to register she was female. Go figure.

As bleak as his mood was, Fergus couldn't resist watching Claire Bryce's retreat to the kitchen. She was a sturdy woman with mouth-watering curves.

Sturdy. Yeah, not a word he'd ever repeat to her, but it was the truth, and this part of her physique made her perfect. Her black hair reached the middle of her back when in its usual braid, and he'd seen her hair loose about her shoulders and fanning over pillows once, a vision that haunted him. Her bright blue eyes held an eagerness for life. They sparkled and laughed and seldom held condemnation or anger while she worked damn hard in this pub of hers, pulling crazy hours to get the pub, restaurant, and accommodation back to a viable business. He'd never once heard her complain, and he admired her drive and determination.

Hell, she occupied his thoughts way too much. Dating another human was asking for trouble, and since there were few paranormal creatures down this end of the country, he remained alone. Although he didn't think she held any prejudice toward the supernatural species, he didn't want to test his gut instinct. He considered her a friend. That had to be enough.

The Australian men wanted another round of drinks, and Fergus rounded the bar to serve them. He'd worked in pubs in Auckland to earn his way before training to become a cop. He'd never mentioned it to Claire, but he didn't mind helping. As he poured the beers, he wondered where Claire's regular bar staff were this afternoon.

Fergus was still busy serving drinks when Claire bustled from the kitchen bearing a tray of meals for the Australian tourists. Her steps slowed, but he gestured her on and continued serving the customers who appeared to have finished a cruise on the lake and had come inside to warm their chilled bones. A few requested soup and he took their orders with efficiency.

"Thank you so much," Claire said. "This is going above and beyond. Remind me not to charge you for your tea tomorrow."

"The couple at the end of the bar wants soup and loaded wedges. The couple here wants coffee and ham sandwiches. I didn't like to touch the coffee machine. You need a license to drive that thing."

Claire laughed, her tinkling amusement easing the tension in his gut. He pulled another pint, took the money, and rang the order on the till. Nearly an hour passed before the rush subsided, and Fergus returned to the customers' side.

"Thank you, Fergus. I can't tell you how much I appreciate this. Charlie is sick, and Pat declared herself in love and rushed to Queenstown. Rachel at the employment agency is confident I'll have a replacement by tomorrow. Do you want something to eat?"

"No, thanks. The tea isn't sitting right as it is, but I needed the caffeine to keep me awake."

Claire stepped up to the coffee machine and soon had it hissing and gurgling to produce a coffee. She pushed the grinder button, and an extra hit of ground coffee beans wafted to him. When another two customers approached the bar, Fergus waved her off and listened to their drinks order.

Claire served the coffee and took more food orders. "Where are these people coming from?" Then she shrugged. "This is always the way. I'm short-staffed for some reason, and Joe Public decides it's the perfect day for a meal at the pub. Not that I'm complaining. Not really. I'm uncomfortable that you're helping me when you're on your break."

Fergus reached over and squeezed her forearm. He'd intended silent commiseration, comfort, or some other brain-fart reason. All he knew was physical contact was a mistake since sparks shot from his fingertips and darted up his arm. A groan escaped him before he jerked away his hand. Claire jolted and gazed at him wide-eyed before a customer signaled her and broke the intimate moment.

Fergus tore his gaze from her, shaken by the physical attraction—the acute awareness coursing through his body. He grabbed a handle, his hands trembling as he filled it with lager. In the small hours, he'd recalled how her body felt sliding against his. Yeah, he knew, and his fingers tingled, craving more contact. Kissing. That was the next step. He glanced at Claire, his gaze grazing her face and coming to rest on her lips. Yeah, kissing. He wanted to lock lips with Claire so badly his entire body vibrated with urgent need.

But his dragon status made anything other than friendship impossible. He'd made that mistake with Miranda and wasn't about to repeat it—lesson learned.

Then, there was the human versus paranormal situation. The New Zealand government's decision to give paranormals equal status had come late last year. Some humans vehemently protested the new laws that granted equality. Fergus appreciated living in a quiet town where tourists visited briefly to hike the Kepler or other famous walking tracks before leaving.

In the larger centers, humans protested with massive marches. One of the gatherings in Auckland had bubbled over into a riot. A man had died in a stampede triggered by firecrackers. The crowd panicked. Over twenty suffered injuries, and property destruction ensued. Those paranormals who'd come out into the open suffered damage to their businesses, stones thrown through windows, and, in some cases, even worse, from fire or water.

Verbal insults were the norm. Even though paranormal folk had worked alongside humans for years without difficulty, suddenly, their human friends and co-workers didn't trust them.

Fergus didn't want that drama. He loved living in Te Anau since he could walk in the mountains and fly in his dragon form whenever the urge struck him. He liked his job and helping people. It was rewarding, and he thought he was good at policing. No, it was best to ignore this unfortunate attraction to Claire.

Claire sent him a smile, and he forced himself not to respond. His dragon sneered at him, but his snarled insult bounced harmlessly away because Fergus was so focused on remaining neutral and out of romantic trouble.

"Things are quieting down. I might head out." His heart flip-flopped at the disappointment flickering over her face, and he ached to hold her. Instead, he put more space between them.

"Thanks for helping me, Fergus."

He dipped his head and shot her an assessing glance before turning for the door. He felt her stare bore into his back, and regret filled him, yet he didn't halt, didn't apologize.

The door flew open before he reached it, and a brown

wolflike dog raced inside. Laughter and joking flowed toward Fergus. A smaller animal, this one gray, shot indoors, running so fast it crashed into Fergus's legs. The dog let out a shrill bark, and a woman with flowing brown and blonde hair darted toward Fergus, scooped up the animal, and cooed to it while stroking its coarse gray fur.

The woman turned in his direction, her friendly smile ratcheting up a notch on seeing Fergus. She beamed.

Fergus's mouth opened and closed while shock did a number on his powers of speech. What the hell?

Aware he was creating a traffic jam, he stepped aside to let several adults enter the pub. Their chatter was full of excitement as if this was the start of a grand adventure.

A tall woman in tight blue jeans, a scarlet blouse, and biker boots strutted through the doorway. Her dark blonde hair was jaw-length in one of those blunt cuts. A tall man with brown hair followed the woman through the door. His brown eyes brightened when he saw Fergus.

"Son," he boomed, and seconds later, Fergus found himself sandwiched between his parents in a tight hug.

"We caught your scent and wondered why you were here," his mother said, patting his cheek. "You've lost weight. Are you eating properly?"

"Yes, Ma," Fergus said. It was no use telling his mother he was in perfect health. She always fussed. "What are you doing here? Why didn't you call and let me know you were coming?" So he could talk them out of the visit.

His mother tossed her head, setting her hair swinging. She flapped her hand. "Pooh! You would've tried to talk us out of it. We wanted to see where you live and meet your friends. I said to Dougal, 'We want a break from Auckland. Why don't we visit Fergus?' Elspeth and Iain were ready for a holiday, and James and Finn announced they were tagging along. Elspeth and Iain brought their two boys. It's time you met your nephews again."

"Excuse me," came a loud voice from behind them.

Claire.

Hell, shock had turned his brain to mush. Slowly, Fergus fought free from his parents' embrace. A sharp poke at his hip had his eyes widening. A dagger? What the hell?

"Hello, pretty lady," his father boomed, casually flicking his shirt to cover the weapon. "What can we do for you?"

"I'm sorry, but it's against health regulations to have dogs inside my pub. You'll have to sit outside in the garden, but I can serve you there," Claire said.

The dogs. Wolves—his two nephews, no doubt.

Fergus opened his mouth to apologize, but his mother beat him to it.

"Oh, no. It's too cold outside. I'd prefer to sit indoors. Dougal, can you please order me a glass of wine? Elspeth, the boys need to change into clothes now."

Fergus started to object, to say something to avoid the calamity that lay ahead, but Iain and Elspeth were already summoning their boys.

"Niall! Connor!" Elspeth said. "It's time to shift."

The wolf pups, who took after their werewolf father instead of their dragon mother, scampered to their parents.

"You should have a sign stating your preference for paranormal creatures to be in their two-legged form," his mother told Claire, chidingly.

Fergus directed his glance to his feet. *Bloody hell.* His day had already been crappy, but now it dive-bombed farther south. His shit day detonated into bedlam.

3

CLAIRE'S BROWS ELEVATED AS she scanned the adults—very attractive smiling men and women—before settling on Fergus. She hadn't meant to eavesdrop, but they were Fergus's family. She glanced at the two rowdy dogs and witnessed a shimmer enveloping the larger one. Her eyes widened, then she winced at the horrid sound of...of...

She blinked, and when she refocused, a naked boy of around six or seven stood where the animal had sat only seconds earlier. The young woman with hair of an identical shade to Fergus's calmly pulled clothes from her large red leather handbag and helped the boy to dress.

"Connor," a man with tousled brown hair said, the tone stern. He had the build of a rugby player with bulging thigh muscles, broad shoulders, and a trim waist. He wasn't as tall as Fergus, but most would need to look up to meet his gaze. "Connor."

Now that she'd inspected the creature at close quarters, she'd concluded that if the animal wasn't a wolf, it was a close cousin. The wolf sat on its haunches and whined.

The man crouched, staring the wolf in the eye. "You can play later. Aren't you hungry?"

The whine transformed, ending with a sharp bark.

"Shift," the man said, a dominant note shimmering in his voice.

Claire froze, her breath caught. That commanding tone made her want to obey, and she shook herself, backing away to observe in safety. The new arrivals intrigued her customers, too. Several huddled together and whispered rapidly, their eyes wide as they studied Fergus and the latest arrivals.

The wolf rose to all fours, and if an animal could frown, this one did. Its furry brows drew together. Its eyes closed, and his entire body tensed, then began to vibrate.

"Sorry about this." The younger woman, who resembled Fergus, inched toward Claire as if she were approaching a wild animal and wasn't confident about its reaction. "Connor is young and needs to focus to start his shift. We were so eager to surprise Fergus that we didn't think about the boys in their wolf forms. Thank you for your understanding."

Claire smiled, and the woman relaxed, returning her smile with a bright and friendly one. Claire hadn't met any paranormal beings in person since Te Anau was a small town, dependent on the tourist trade and the locals all human, but her instincts told her this woman had received hostile reactions in the past. It was understandable on

44

one level because the paranormal folk had strength and abilities that humans had no hope of countering. But they'd lived secretly amongst the human population for centuries without a kerfuffle. And...

Her gaze snapped toward Fergus. Did this mean that Fergus—their local cop and the man she'd toppled halfway in love with—wasn't human? Holy cow! And...and she'd slept with him.

Wow! She hadn't suspected a thing.

"Where are you staying?" Fergus asked the older couple.

Claire's fascinated gaze drifted to the child still in his wolf form, to the other child, to the adults, and Fergus. Fergus refused to acknowledge her, but she wasn't dumb. Double wow! This explained so much. His private nature. His caution.

Despite the open presence of numerous paranormal beings, she understood the desire for secrecy. Although it was unreasonable, a sector of the population believed them untrustworthy and dangerous. In Fergus's case, the Te Anau residents would believe him to be fair and do a stellar job—at least she hoped so.

"We've hired a house for two weeks with an option of longer should we decide to stay. Son, you understated the beauty of this place. It's easy to understand why you enjoy living in Te Anau. Look at all this open space!" the older woman exclaimed, spreading her arms wide. "The mountains. The lake. The incredible breathtaking views."

Claire studied the older couple more closely and noted their similarities to Fergus. They were tall, athletic, and had the same effortless ease of movement.

Fergus broke the momentary silence. "I've got to go since we've had some trouble here this morning, but I'll catch up with you tonight around six," Fergus said. "Iain, I could do with your expertise since you're here."

"Will it take long?" Iain asked. "James and Finn should arrive later. I want to give them instructions before I let them loose on the single ladies around town."

The color faded from Fergus's cheeks. "Should I expect the cousins or any of the gargoyles?" he asked, his voice low and hoarse as if he'd received a shock.

His mother pursed her lips. Something shifted behind her eyes, her pupils narrowing to a vertical line. Claire blinked, her mind telling her she was seeing things while her heart soared at meeting paranormal creatures. Was Fergus a wolf? Claire slid her attention toward Fergus and found he was watching her instead of his parents.

"Mother," he said, still watching Claire. "Is anyone else intending to visit me?"

"Perhaps," his mother said with a tinkling laugh. "It depends on the situation at home."

Fergus wrenched his gaze from Claire's and scowled at his mother. "What situation?"

"The locals we used to exchange good mornings with and the occasional barbecue are suddenly upset to learn they have dragons and wolves for neighbors." The woman's lip curled in disdain, and her husband slipped his arm around her waist in silent comfort. "Life has become more difficult in Auckland, son. It's not so bad at the farm, but we wanted a respite."

Something in her neutral tone told Claire this was

an understatement, and sympathy flooded her. Claire understood how some humans might react to suddenly learning their neighbors shifted to other creatures. The fear of the unknown persisted despite the paranormal species having no prior troubles before the new equality laws. A sector of the population was seeing danger where there was none.

Fergus heaved a sigh. "I've gotta go. I'll call you later."

"You'll have dinner with us," his father spoke up for the first time. "We haven't seen you for months, not since last Christmas."

"Elspeth and I will cook dinner," his mother said. "Bring wine. Something local."

Fergus's face softened, and he closed the distance between him and his parents. He hugged his mother and kissed her cheek. He embraced his father too, then murmured something Claire couldn't hear and stalked from the pub, the children's father trailing him.

"Can we get a drink or not?" the impatient local builder called out, clearly tired of waiting.

"Yes, of course." Claire scuttled behind the bar, filled a pint tankard with dark beer, and handed it to the builder. "Sorry about that," she said brightly. "It's not every day you see a wolf running around the pub interior."

The builder grunted, handed over several coins, and retreated to a corner to read his newspaper. A man of many words. *Not.*

"Do you not have any paranormal species around here?" Fergus's mother asked, overhearing Claire's words.

Color heated Claire's cheeks, and she gasped. "I didn't

mean to sound rude."

Fergus's mother made a pooh-poohing sound. "No offense taken. I'm Fiona Murray. This is my husband, Dougal. In case you haven't figured it out, we're Fergus's parents."

"Claire," she said. "I'm pleased to meet you. What can I get you to drink?"

"I'll have a glass of dry white wine. Something local," Fiona said. "Dougal?"

"A lager for me, please. It's mighty hot out there today," Dougal replied. "I thought it was early spring."

"It was cold last week," Claire said as she poured the drinks. "Enjoy this weather while you can."

"Yes, we should go for a flight to get our bearings," Fiona suggested.

Claire started, fumbling the pint glass under the tap and spilling beer before she righted it. They were going to fly. Hadn't they mentioned dragons? Her mind conjured several dragons wheeling through the sky above the lake.

"I checked, and you have float planes and a small airport," Dougal said to Claire. "Is that correct?"

"Yes," Claire agreed, waiting with fascination. They were like a regular family with rambunctious children and interesting dynamics.

The younger woman—Fergus's sister—hustled up to the bar. "Are you still doing food? The boys will settle once they eat. My sons do better with regular meals."

"This is my daughter, Elspeth. Her husband, Iain, disappeared with Fergus," Fiona said.

"I'm short-staffed, but I can make toasted sandwiches, a

48

bowl of wedges, or fries for you," Claire offered.

"That's perfect," Elspeth said. "We'll take two toasted ham and cheese sandwiches and three bowls of wedges."

"Right," Claire said. "Did you and the children want drinks? I'll organize them before I get the food underway. Please shout through the hatch if anyone requires a drink."

"No problem, darlin'," Dougal said.

Claire poured another glass of wine and two lemonades for the kids, her mind awhirl with thoughts of Fergus and what type of creature he turned into when he shifted. Would it be rude to ask his parents? Yes. Yes, it would. But she could ask Fergus when she saw him next, and she couldn't wait to quiz him. Why had Fergus kept this a secret? Most locals were easygoing, although the town was a minefield of gossip. All they wanted was a committed cop who maintained peace in their community. They didn't care about color or race or species. At least, that's what she hoped.

Yes, there was trouble in some places, and she'd watched news items on TV where anxious neighbors were upset and uneasy about the weird sounds coming from their neighbors' properties. Some parents didn't want their children to mix with *others*.

Once she'd dispersed the drinks and taken payment, she hustled to the kitchen and pulled frozen wedges from the freezer. The children—now in human form—behaved far better than many kids who visited for family meals.

Claire let out a groan and started building sandwiches. While the knowledge of paranormal blood might disturb many women, Claire had liked Fergus before his parents' arrival. The new information only increased her fascination levels.

"Claire!"

Claire strode to the food hatch and smiled at the regular customer, a retired bank manager. "What's up, Ernie?"

"A young lady has arrived from the employment agency," he said.

"Ask her to sit at the bar. I'll join her in a few minutes."

Ernie issued a cheerful shout of acknowledgment. "Right, you are, lass."

Claire finished cooking the wedges and plated them before adding sweet chili sauce and sour cream. She retrieved the toasties from her sandwich machine, cut them into triangles, and arranged them on a plate before carrying everything to the serving hatch. When she arrived at the other side, she noticed three people waiting for drinks.

"I'm sorry to keep you waiting." Claire thought quickly and marched over to the young dark-haired woman sitting in the far corner. "Are you here about the job?"

"Yes."

"What is your name?"

"Valerie Benz."

"Right, Valerie. I want you to go behind the bar and serve the waiting customers."

"I don't know the prices."

"Tell them it's their lucky day. Since I've kept them waiting, I'll give them a free drink. Once I deliver this food, I'll come to help you, and we'll see about this job interview."

"Okay," Valerie said and headed for the customers.

The girl's tidy appearance in a denim skirt, a plain black T-shirt and her hair pulled into a neat ponytail had already impressed Claire. She had a friendly smile and met Claire's gaze during their conversation. Things were looking up. She plucked two bowls of wedges from the serving hatch and hurried to the Murray family group.

"I'm sorry for the delay. Murphy's Law says it's always busy when you're short-staffed."

"If you need someone else short-term, my brother James has bar experience," Elspeth said. "He was muttering about getting a job earlier in the week."

"All right," Claire said. "Tell him to come and see me."

Claire legged it back to the bar to check on Valerie. The young woman had served the three men and taken their money since they had the correct change. "Thank you," Claire said, and since no customers were waiting, she discussed wages and hours.

"That's perfect," Valerie said. "Although I'm only here for a few months. I wanted to see the country before I start university in March next year."

Used to the transitory nature of her employees, Claire merely nodded. "Can you stay and work today, or do you have other commitments?"

"No, I can work. Should I clear the tables for you?"

"Thank you." Bonus! An employee who thought for herself without prompting. "If possible, I'd like you to work for the entire week. You can have off Mondays and Tuesdays."

"That's fine," Valerie said. "Although I'm eager to save

money, so I want to work as many hours as you can give me."

Claire nodded. "We'll talk later."

Two young men walked into the bar, and the Murray group hailed them with cries of welcome. Claire smiled, enjoying the closeness of the family, and served yet another customer. Busy days had become rare since the pandemic, and she planned to make the most of it.

Valerie settled in fast, picking up Claire's systems easily. Right now, she was chatting with one of Claire's regulars, but Claire noticed her gaze kept going to Fergus's family. Not that Claire could blame her since the young males were serious eye candy. Maybe hiring one would increase business. Single men were a rarity around Te Anau.

Fergus cursed under his breath as he stomped from the pub to his vehicle, with Iain hustling to keep up behind him. Thankfully, his brother-in-law was smart and sensed now wasn't the time to ask questions.

Instead of the brief visit with Claire soothing him, his gut jumped as if he'd eaten inferior quality food. Why had his family chosen to show up during this crucial case? Not only had they arrived unexpectedly, but they had no plans to remain inconspicuous. No, they'd announce their otherness to anyone with eyes or ears. It'd surprise him if the gossip wasn't already ramping up. So much for him blending with the human population.

"I suggested calling you first," Iain said in a mild voice,

thankfully misinterpreting his mood as anger at his family for outing him. "But your parents are stubborn once they make a decision."

Fergus gritted his teeth at the reminder. He'd seen the locals giving him a side-eye. Not everyone would take the news well, resulting in potential repercussions. Sighing, he unlocked his police vehicle and jumped behind the wheel. He waited for Iain to clamber inside before he drove to Nikau's surgery.

"Why are we visiting a vet?" Iain asked when they pulled up in the parking lot.

"You'll see," Fergus said, stopping at the front desk. "I'd prefer you to form your own impressions before I give you details."

Iain gave a curt nod. Fergus liked and respected his brother-in-law, and frankly, his unexpected appearance was the one good thing about this mess.

"Nikau told me to tell you to go inside as soon as you arrived. This way." The tall, thin vet nurse had a strawberry-blonde ponytail and wore a blue lab coat. Although she was pretty and no doubt caught many a male eye, she didn't flirt with him. Fergus appreciated her professionalism. It was a pity he hadn't recognized the provocative trait in Miranda before she'd reeled him in and ground his heart into dust.

The nurse knocked on a door halfway down the corridor, then opened it for Fergus and Iain to enter. At Fergus's nod of thanks, she offered a quick smile and retreated.

"Nikau, this is my brother-in-law, Iain. I've roped him

in to help me with this investigation." Fergus shut the door behind them and stepped nearer but didn't get too close because he didn't want to introduce new DNA and confuse matters.

Iain lost his lazy amusement, his nostrils flaring, his wolfish senses feeding him information. His gaze narrowed, but he remained silent. Fergus inclined his head and turned his attention back to Nikau.

"Pleased to meet you," Nikau said, extending his hand.

Iain shook the vet's hand. "Likewise."

"Any progress?" Fergus asked, impatient to get past the niceties.

"Samuel died from a knife wound to the heart, as we expected. Judging from the wound, the weapon was long and thin. A stiletto blade. Apart from that, Samuel was in reasonable shape. He's a fraction underweight, but from memory, he's increased his weight from last year."

"I tried to ensure he had regular meals. He had put on weight and was doing better since he moved into the cottage at the back of my place. Can you tell me anything else?"

"He fought hard. I discovered blood in his claws and a fragment of purple fabric. I also found a few hairs, but I'm having trouble identifying them."

"So you think that another paranormal creature killed him?"

Nikau lifted his head to study Fergus, his brown gaze steady and intent. "I'm not sure what to think. There's something else." He reached for a jar containing a purple fly. The agitated insect repeatedly thumped against the jar, flinging its body against the glass prison in its attempt to escape. "These aren't insects. They're a sort of mechanical bug, but they function like flies. It was lucky you covered Samuel; otherwise, I doubt I'd have much body to study. The flies appear to function as scavengers."

"They're not insects?" Iain asked, craning his neck for a better view. "Can I see?"

At Fergus's nod, Iain picked up the jar and studied the agitated fly at close range.

Fergus tapped the fingers of his right hand against his thigh while trying to make sense of this latest puzzle. He had to do his best for Samuel, even if the town council sacked him for concealing his species type. "You think that whoever killed Samuel released these flies to clean up after them?"

"I do," Nikau said. "The flies ate through the lower part of the sheet and attacked his leg. They destroyed a sizeable chunk before we transported Samuel here."

"Is there anything else you can tell us?" Fergus asked.

"Nothing at the moment," Nikau said. "I need to wait for test results, which might take some time. The lab is frantically busy, as usual."

"Any estimate on how long it will take to identify the species of those hairs you found?" Fergus asked.

"I've done a quick search and have found nothing yet." Nikau met his gaze, his eyes full of sympathy. "I'm sorry, Fergus, but we might never learn what happened to Samuel."

"Unless whoever did the deed repeats the crime," Iain said, saying what Fergus was trying not to think.

"Yes," Nikau agreed somberly.

"Hell." Fergus dragged his hand through his hair, trying to think what to do. He had to keep the residents safe, and he owed it to Samuel to discover his murderer and bring them to justice.

"I'll do everything I can to help," Nikau said, repeating his words from earlier.

"And me," Iain said without hesitation.

"Thanks." The buzz of a fly snared Fergus's attention. "What do we do about the flies? Do you think they are dangerous to the town's residents?"

"They appear to eat carrion, so our citizens should be safe enough." Nikau turned to study the angry insect, still trying to burrow through the glass. "But that's an educated guess. An older person or a child might not survive if a swarm attacked them. As far as I can see, there are no manufacturer's marks or identification. Haven't heard of anything similar, either. Have you?"

"No," Fergus said. "I'll poke around and check with other police departments." He paused, thinking. "Better take photos to send with my request."

"I have some dead ones over here," Nikau said, pointing to a stainless steel shelf. "At least, I don't think they'll come back to life. It's hard to tell. You can take that live one with you, but I wouldn't suggest releasing it."

Fergus studied the purple flies Nikau indicated and snapped several photos.

Iain eyed them closely. "How can you tell they're manmade?"

Nikau gestured at a microscope. "Look at the one on the

slide. Seeing the difference from a real fly is difficult unless you study them through a microscope."

Iain dipped his head to look at the slide, his swift intake of air making Nikau chuckle.

"That was my initial reaction. I have no idea how they're made because the work is intricate. It might pay to check that none found a way into your house. Better to be safe."

"Do we know of any specialist bug men?" Iain asked.

"I have a friend in Australia who might help," Nikau said. "But it's gonna take time."

Fergus scowled, not liking what Nikau was telling him. "Someone must know what these things are."

"I took a quick lunch break earlier and checked the internet. I couldn't find anything remotely close."

"That's not good," Fergus muttered, his mind racing ahead. It was apparent his boss didn't care about the death of an old werewolf. His boss didn't understand that Samuel had fought in the Middle East and kept people safe. He'd helped at the border during the worst of the COVID pandemic when anti-vaxxers had resorted to violence to retain their freedoms. Although the war had affected Samuel's mind, he was still a decent citizen. All he'd wanted was a purpose and a roof over his head.

No, Samuel hadn't deserved this death, and Fergus intended to do everything he could to bring the culprit down and make him accountable.

4

THE COTTAGE HIS PARENTS had rented was on the lake and commanded views of the distant mountains. A fantastic location. He knocked on the door, and his father answered mere seconds later. Fergus grinned at a flash of memory. He'd never successfully sneaked anywhere as a teenager since his parents possessed hearing to rival a bat's.

"Fergus, my boy," his father boomed and drew him into a tight embrace.

At that moment, Fergus admitted to himself he'd missed his family even with all the messy emotions that came with them. His parents and siblings disagreed with his stance on retaining his privacy. They saw no reason to stay hidden while other paranormal beings in New Zealand were openly enjoying life and shifting more frequently.

They didn't understand the unspoken enmity that ran through the entire chain of command within the police force since the new laws had worsened. He loved his job and helping people. He could retain his position if he kept to himself and carried out his duties. The head-in-the-sand approach had worked well until his family's exposure today. He wanted to be angry, but he really was pleased to see his parents.

"Fiona and Elspeth have prepared a fine dinner. Since the evening is so mild, we're having a barbecue in the garden. Fergus, my boy, you've picked a stunning place to plant your feet. We plan to take a flight later tonight. Do you have time to show us the sights from the air?"

Fergus hesitated before nodding. "Sure, Dad."

Any astute person would've worked out his paranormal secret today. It wouldn't be long before the nosy questions started. It would make his job harder and his position within the community complex, but he'd deal with it and continue doing his best to serve the people of Te Anau.

"How long do you intend to stay? I'm investigating a murder at present and won't be able to spend much time with you."

"Murder?" His father ushered him deeper into the cottage. "Iain didn't say anything."

Fergus appreciated his brother-in-law's discreetness. He stepped past his father into a tiled vestibule that gave way to a vast open space with enormous picture windows facing the lake. He'd never visited this rental, and the interior was more spacious than he'd assumed from the outside of the building. Double doors opened onto a wooden deck extending the living area. Beyond, a large expanse of grass continued down toward the lake. The kitchen occupied one corner with a long breakfast bar suitable for a family.

"Great place," Fergus said. "How many bedrooms are there?"

"Four," his mother said, coming over to kiss Fergus on the cheek. "It's a bit of a squeeze with us all here, but we've pitched a tent outside, and James and Finn have claimed that. My theory is it's so they can sneak in and out without us noticing."

Fergus snorted, and his parents winked in concert. "Good luck to them." He doubted his younger brother or Iain's brother would skulk away without his parents noticing.

"Murder?" his father prompted.

Fergus sighed, hating the yank back to reality. "Yeah. We rarely have trouble in Te Anau. The most I usually deal with is drunk and disorderly, teens driving at speed, or search and rescue when a trekker is late returning from the mountains. This murder is worrying. I'm alone because they're busy at Invercargill and can't spare the men."

"Ah, that's why you wanted Iain's help," Dougal said.

His mother squeezed his biceps. "I have confidence in you, son. You're smart and have an excellent eye for detail. With Iain's help, I'm sure you'll get results."

"Thanks." Unusual emotion welled in Fergus, knotting his throat, and he was lucky he'd squeezed that much out. Used to a solitary lifestyle since he'd split with Miranda, he usually carried the burden on his own. He had no one to discuss work matters or brainstorm ideas with. He thought of Claire for a moment before forcing the wayward notion away. "Dad, what's up with the dagger?

You can't wear that in public."

His father squared his shoulders, determination settling on his face. "We told you about Seth and the problems he and Malikah had. I could've done with a weapon then. That debacle made me decide to purchase Betty."

"Betty?"

"My dagger."

"But you can't wear it—Betty—in town. It's not legal. The locals have enough to gossip about without adding a weapon."

"Don't worry, boy. The witches spelled her for me. Only non-humans will see her."

Hell, he needed to sit down. "A warning, Dad. If I hear a scrap of gossip around town about your weapon, I'll confiscate Betty."

His father's chin rose, but before he could argue, his mother broke in, changing the subject with adroitness.

"Did Dougal tell you we're going for a flight after dinner? Join us." Excitement glittered in his mother's sparkling eyes.

"Sure," Fergus said. "Although I'm positive the Te Anau residents aren't ready for a thunder of dragons soaring over the lake."

"They'll be used to seeing you," his sister called from the kitchen, her hands deftly shaping a loaf of bread dough.

Even though he knew his family wouldn't understand, he led with the truth. "Until you came today, no one suspected I wasn't human. It's a habit to hide my identity, and since there was only one werewolf in the area, it seemed more practical to keep the status quo."

"Son, your ancestors would turn in their graves," his mother snapped. "We've been gifted with this opportunity to live with openness and truth as we used to hundreds of years ago. If the humans can't accept us, that's their problem, not ours."

"Fiona, leave the boy alone," Dougal said. "Come outside for a walk and a smooch."

"But our son is hiding his identity," Fiona said with anger in her tone. "It's not right. We must stand up for our rights. Our government has made it illegal for humans to torment or belittle us because of our otherness. Where would we be if every paranormal creature remained hidden like Fergus?"

"Fiona," Dougal said. "Leave it."

"But it's not right," his mother insisted as his father led her outside onto the deck.

"Ma is right," Elspeth said.

"You don't think I have the right to make this decision in my own time?" Fergus asked, glaring at his sister. "Because I am pissed. I love you all, but you don't know what the fallout might be for me and my job. Now, along with this murder, I'll have to deal with scared residents and more covert glances than usual. I don't want to argue with you or Mum and Dad, but what you've done is wrong."

Elspeth scowled. "But—"

"Leave Fergus alone, Elspeth," Iain said. "We each decide how we go on in this world, which is what I tried to tell you and your parents before we descended on Fergus. You know how difficult living openly in Auckland is, so you shouldn't be so hard on your brother. What do you need me to do? Cook the meat? I'm sure Fergus won't mind helping me barbecue."

Elspeth washed her hands and dried them on a towel. "Fergus, I'm sorry. You're right, and my only excuse is that I missed you, and you kept putting us off when we wanted to visit. That's why Mum dug in her toes and was so determined to come. She wanted to see you in person. Do you think you'll face repercussions?"

Fergus softened a fraction. He *was* glad to see them, but he wished they'd arrived in a more clandestine manner. "I don't know."

"Sorry," Elspeth said. "I'll do anything I can to help you."

"I know," Fergus said. "Right now, I'm hungry."

"Oh! The salads are ready. The potatoes are parboiled. I'll wrap them in foil, and you can finish cooking them on the barbecue at a low heat. The bread will take around half an hour. The steaks are marinating now."

"All right. We'll grab a beer and fire up the barbecue. Give us a shout when you're ready for us to put on the potatoes, and one of us will come inside to collect them," Iain said.

Wisely, Fergus remained silent and let Iain speak with his wife. The practicalities of preparing dinner seemed to ease her mood, although he was certain either his mother or sister or both would raise the subject again. Hell, he'd already lost Miranda because she wasn't willing to marry a dragon. That she'd married another man and kept calling him whenever she was miserable only reinforced his desire to keep his business private. He preferred to avoid curious women seeking a brief adventure to boast about later.

"Want a beer?" Iain asked.

"Sure. Where is the barbecue? I'll get it started."

"Outside on the deck to the left," Iain replied.

Fergus left Iain to sweet-talk his wife and strode outside. After he'd dropped Iain off, he'd gone over the scene again. Not that he'd discovered anything new. Fergus had searched Samuel's cabin, but it had been tidy and undisturbed. Whoever had killed Samuel had done it in the garden before vanishing. By the time he'd arrived back at his place, even the flies had gone. That was weird—the way they'd suddenly appeared and then vanished.

The barbecue area caught his eye, matching the cottage's neat and stylish design. When Iain arrived with the beers and a bowl of foil-wrapped potatoes, Fergus had the cover off the barbecue and the gas burning. "A low heat, right?"

"Yeah."

Something his mother said gnawed at him. "Have you been having trouble at home? I heard there have been marches and isolated incidents in Auckland. I don't recall any of the disturbances being near you."

"The kids get a hard time at school from their fellow students," Iain said. "Some clients I'd worked security jobs for canceled their contracts once they learned I was a werewolf. Everyone is on edge and looking at each other sideways. You can feel the tension in the air, and it's gonna boil over soon despite the new equality laws."

"Yet you traveled openly through the rest of the countryside," Fergus said.

Iain chuckled. "Yeah. Makes no sense but it has been good for the boys. For all of us."

"Do you have a plan?"

"That's part of the reason we decided to take a vacation," Iain said. "We thought it might allow things to settle if we left for a month, and meanwhile, we could decide on our future."

"Are you thinking of relocating?"

"Possibly. Elspeth needs an opportunity to use her degree. She has been talking about making gin with native botanicals and is using this trip to collect specimens and scout locations. We're happy at the farm, but as much as I adore your parents, we'd love our own place."

"Understandable. What do you think of Te Anau?"

"The setting is gorgeous, and the people have been welcoming. The woman at the pub went out of her way to make the boys something to eat."

"Claire?"

"If she's the woman you were devouring with your eyes when we arrived."

Fergus neither confirmed nor denied, not willing to let Iain tease answers from him. Hell, had he been that transparent? Not good. Wanting to occupy his hands, he plucked the potatoes from the bowl and set them on the hot plate.

"Not talking, huh?"

"I'm too busy for women."

Iain's hand closed on Fergus's biceps. "You're not still hung up on Miranda?"

"Hell no!" Fergus didn't hide his horror.

"Glad to hear it. Elspeth didn't think she was right for you."

"Elspeth and Miranda butted heads," Fergus said, tension flooding into his voice. Looking his mistakes in the eye unsettled his dragon and rattled them both. Not a brilliant combination, so he changed the subject. "What about Elspeth's job?"

"She's in a better position than me because her boss is a fae. He doesn't stand for nonsense, and when one of his human workers starts giving the paranormal workers a hard time, he threatens to do a spell to make warts appear on his nose. One dude didn't believe he could, but when he continued harassing the rest of the staff, the boss started his spell. A bright lime-green wart grew on the tip of his nose. In a fit of anger, he stormed out of the building, vowing to report the fae man for using magic against a human. He didn't realize the spell was temporary, and by the time he reached the police station, the wart had disappeared. He had what looked like lime green paint on his nose."

Fergus snorted. "An excellent trick to play on the drunken tourists I occasionally deal with. They enjoy celebrating and sometimes get carried away after finishing a long walk. Sam always told me I should shift and bite them." Fergus paused to take a breath, pain arcing through his chest. His heart ached for the werewolf who'd made his home here. That someone had murdered him when he was finally stilling his devils didn't seem fair. Hell, it was horrendous.

Fergus gripped his beer can and tried to sort out his

thoughts—to think like a police officer rather than a friend. "I've examined the scene and found nothing amiss. There was a footprint, which I photographed. The weird purple flies and the as-yet-unidentified hairs. I couldn't locate anything else unusual, but I wondered if you could have a sniff around the garden. Your nose is better than mine."

Iain met Fergus's gaze, and the wolf's eyes displayed silent sympathy. "We're here for at least two weeks. Elspeth will probably be glad that I'm keeping busy."

"Mum and Dad are determined to fly after dinner. Why don't we check out my place after we've eaten? It won't take long, then you'll be back here for babysitting duties."

Iain groaned then brightened. "I should get our brothers to babysit the kids for an hour. Yeah, we'll do that. I know where you live. You fly with your family. They won't let up until you do."

"You make a good point," Fergus said drily.

"You documented everything, right?"

"Yeah, I've looked over the scene three times today and taken photos. Whoever killed Samuel didn't enter his cabin or my house. They stabbed him in the garden and left."

"Is your back garden locked?"

"It is as of today, but I can give you my house keys, and you can enter the garden from my kitchen."

"Done," Iain said. "Hopefully, I'll have something to report when you return from your flight."

"Thanks." Fergus handed over his keys, and Iain pocketed them.

One of the regulars burst inside the pub, his breathing harsh. He bent at the waist and dragged in huge, raspy breaths. "Quick! There are four dragons flying over the lake. Four black dragons."

"Have you been drinking?" another regular asked, his glass suspended in mid-air.

"No! See for yourself. Dragons, I tell you!" Red-faced, he squeezed out the words before gasping for air again.

Claire didn't hesitate. After swiftly exiting the door, she abruptly halted by a table of customers, captivated by the sight. Four dragons flew in formation, occasionally one breaking off to swoop low over the lake. One spurted flames, illuminating the twilight shadows with a burst of light.

"Did you see that?" a skinny retiree in jeans cried. She removed her glasses, cleaned them with the hem of her cotton shirt, and pushed them back onto her nose. Her mouth fell open to reveal stained yellow teeth. "Don't that beat all?"

Claire didn't answer, instead watching the dragons. Despite their size, they were graceful, their flight unhurried as if enjoying an evening stroll.

"Who are they?" someone asked once the dragons disappeared behind a mountain range.

Claire didn't respond, even though she suspected she knew. She returned to the pub and started clearing empty plates and glasses from tables. While she listened to the buzz of excited conversation and heard various opinions ranging from disgust to admiration, she didn't add fuel to the fire by telling everyone she was positive one of the dragons was their community cop.

Unfortunately, a regular who'd witnessed the two boys charging around the pub interior in their wolf forms spoke up. "It was those folks who came to visit Fergus," he declared, his face turning red when he found himself the center of attention. It could've been the alcohol since he'd consumed a few pints tonight.

An instant later, the focus of the local customers turned to Claire.

"Do you know something?" Betty, the supermarket proprietor, asked. Her steel-gray curls sat atop her head like a helmet while her pale blue eyes narrowed in determination.

Claire shrugged. "I don't gossip about my customers."

"But they're strangers," Betty objected. "Not locals."

"My rule is for every customer," Claire said firmly and stalked off with a handful of dirty dishes. She cleared the kitchen before returning to help Valerie behind the bar. The girl excelled at her work and was already popular with customers.

Two young men confidently approached the bar. Claire recognized one. He'd been with Fergus's family. When she glanced at the other young man, the resemblance to Fergus was unmistakable.

The two men disregarded the dragon talk and focused on ordering drinks and flirting with Valerie. Under their gentle teasing, Valerie lost some of the impassive mask she'd donned ever since her arrival.

Claire backed off to watch the subtle dance of male and female. Then she sighed. If only Fergus was more receptive to romance. Although dozens of eligible men were passing through the town, not one of them was close to Fergus. The truth—she'd rather go without male companionship than settle. She knew her heart, and her heart wanted Fergus.

5

ON HIS RETURN FROM the family outing, energy and confidence fizzed through his veins. A long flight always settled his angst but flying with other dragons and especially his family had invigorated him.

Once Fergus and the others had dressed, they settled down for a supper of steak and salad sandwiches and apple pie for dessert. The mood was one of celebration.

"Fergus, it's easy to see why you've settled here in Te Anau," his mother said. "The air is mountain-fresh. The beautiful lake and craggy peaks are irresistible to any dragon."

"Yeah, all you need is a treasure trove," Iain quipped.

Fergus grinned, basking in his parents' approval. They'd voiced loud opposition when he'd first mentioned his intention to move from the Auckland region, where he'd lived his entire life until he moved to Wellington for his police training. Even his explanations that there were limited jobs available in Auckland hadn't been acceptable to his mother. Miranda lived in Auckland now, and after her marriage to the property tycoon, he'd wanted distance between them. Te Anau had become his haven.

"I'm glad you're enjoying Te Anau. What are you intending to do tomorrow?"

"We'll book a trip on the old sailing ship to see the hidden lakes," his mother said. "The day after, we'll visit the glow worm caves."

"Excellent choices," Fergus said. "You could go fishing or do a day trip to Milford or Doubtful Sounds. You could also walk part of the Kepler Track or the Milford or Routeburn Tracks. I can recommend a company to organize that for you."

His family burst into loud chatter, all talking over each other with a lively discussion of their coming week. With everyone distracted, he signaled for Iain to meet him in the kitchen.

"How did it go?" he asked, tension sliding through him as reality intruded. A murderer mingled with innocents in his town.

"I picked up a faint scent. It's unusual and one I haven't encountered before."

"Can you describe it for me? My nose is more sensitive than average. I noticed a gamey scent, but it didn't lead anywhere."

Iain nodded, his brow creased. "The scent was faint, suggesting someone had a masking skill. A musky odor. Imagine a lump of meat on the turn. That is the best comparison."

"Where did you notice the scent? How did they enter the property?"

"My best guess is they came over the wall," Iain said. "They didn't stay for long."

"They'd staked out my place," Fergus said, irritated because he hadn't suspected a watcher, let alone noticed one.

Iain nodded. "That's my guess. They stabbed your friend and left."

"I don't lock my house. There's no need. Did they walk through the property to leave? Nothing screamed odd or foreign."

"I detected a faint aroma by your kitchen door, but not inside your house." He paused and frowned. "I mentioned the scent seemed masked, which is odd. High emotions always intensify a scent. That could be why I noticed it outside, near where you found Samuel."

Fergus stared at Iain. "That means the murderer could have gone anywhere on my property, and I wouldn't know."

"Yes," Iain conceded. "Sorry I couldn't be more helpful."

"Did you see any flies in the garden?"

"No, there was nothing out of place. I got a whiff of blood and the mystery scent, which is to be expected, but that was all."

Fergus nodded. "I appreciate this."

"You know I'll help if I can."

"Thanks. This is frustrating—the lack of clues, I mean."

"What about specialist cops to help?" Iain asked.

Fergus scowled. "The moment my boss heard it was a paranormal murder, he told me they were short-staffed, and I was on my own."

"That doesn't reflect well on a government department advocating for equality."

"Tell me about it." Fergus released a weary sigh. "Anyone—human or paranormal—with half a brain could've informed the government the law changes wouldn't be seamless. You can't legislate to account for idiots. The different factions are already grumbling. You can't force everyone to do the right thing."

"Yup," Iain agreed. "Is it safe for me to run in the mountains?"

"I'd take care if you intend to run close to the lake. Why don't you get Elspeth to fly you to the Luxmore Hut? You could run part of the Kepler track and get Elspeth to meet you with a picnic. Have a romantic outing. Mum and Dad won't mind watching the boys."

Iain beamed at him. "And you've repaid me for the hour I took to study the crime scene. Elspeth will love that idea. Please, let me pretend I thought of it all on my own."

"Deal," Fergus said.

Saturday. Five days later.

Claire checked the five rooms above the pub to ensure they were guest-ready. She ran her finger over a bedside cabinet. Not a speck of dust. The towels hung neatly on the en suite rail, and the toilet paper hung in a crisp V.

Everything was perfect. Valerie had done an excellent job and prepped the rooms to her satisfaction. She returned downstairs, pleased with her hire.

Customers—locals and tourists—packed the pub, and she jumped behind the bar to help Valerie and Jared, a part-timer, serve drinks.

"Wow, it's busy," she said to Valerie. "It's been busy all week. Not that I'm complaining."

"From what I understand, everyone is flocking here hoping to see the dragons or wolves," Valerie replied.

Claire frowned. "Can they not see them sitting right in front of them?"

Valerie passed two beer handles to a customer, accepting a twenty-dollar note from the man. She handed back the change, remarking, "They know who they are, but customers want to see them shift. The Murray family isn't performing on request."

"I see. Oh, well. I guess I should enjoy the increased patronage while it's around. The family is nice. I like them. They're always polite and ignore the morons who've tried to rile them. Unlike the idiotic picketers at the police station, they don't cause trouble."

"I've heard customers talking big, but it's all bravado. Meeting a wolf or a dragon would terrify them." Valerie smiled, although the amusement didn't reach her eyes, raising Claire's curiosity again. She didn't talk about herself much, only saying she was saving to attend university. She wanted to be a teacher like her parents. Most young girls of Valerie's age were all about themselves, and information tumbled from them, either verbally or via social media. Claire's nosiness had gotten the better of her, and she'd searched for Valerie online. Her employee didn't have an online presence. Valerie did her job well and was already popular with the customers, but Claire wondered about the girl's background.

The rush subsided a little.

"I'll collect the empties while there's a lull," Valerie said. "We were busy early on, and I haven't cleared the floor for ages."

"I'll help," Claire said.

She greeted her customers as she navigated the packed room.

"Hello, Claire," Fiona Murray said.

"You're turning into my best customers," Claire said, a genuine smile curving her lips. Fergus's family was delightful, which was more than she could say about Fergus. Before his parents had arrived, she'd seen him daily for lunch. After the main lunch rush, he'd come and have tea and sometimes a toasted sandwich. Even if he didn't return her feelings, she'd thought they had a friendship. *Apparently not.* The wretched man had started eating lunch and grabbing tea at other town establishments.

Claire plucked several empties from the Murrays' table before moving on to the next—a group of backpackers.

She chatted with them for a few minutes, wanting to encourage them to return during their visit. Since the pandemic, backpackers had become a rare breed. Claire set the glasses at the far end of the bar near the glass-washing machine before hustling away to collect more empties and dirty plates.

With half of the pub done, she wandered outside to check if Valerie required help. One glance told her Valerie was fine and had cleared most of the used glasses. Her laughter rang out as she flirted with the two young men who'd come with Fergus's family. Hearing the young woman relaxing and participating in an innocent flirtation was lovely. A group left, and Claire returned inside to take a meal order.

Fergus's family left with cheerful shouts of farewell, and Claire's temper rose a notch. What on earth was wrong with Fergus? Did he think she thought less of him because she'd discovered his dragon status? She was aware of the whispers circulating. Some locals professed shock. Though there were a few vocal critics, everyone agreed Fergus excelled as their community cop. Not one of them could fault his performance and professionalism. He never put a foot wrong in his involvement with the public and dealt rapidly with any visitors who caused trouble.

But that didn't mean she wasn't angry with him.

He... Heck! She was clueless about what was churning in his brain. Although, to be fair, he was busy with his murder investigation. His family had confirmed that.

Claire grimaced. The locals voiced their own opinions on the matter. The community sat divided, some protesting their tax-payer dollars spent on investigating the death of a man who'd lived on the street.

"Service!" The stranger waved his hands as if Claire were deaf and her eyesight deficient.

"Good afternoon," Claire said, biting back her retort because rudeness wasn't good for business. "Can I get you a drink?"

"A glass of wine. Do you have a French chardonnay?"

"No, but we have excellent local varieties. Our extensive selection pleasantly surprises most people."

The man sniffed—now that Claire was closer, she'd decided he was a salesman instead of a tourist—tugged at the hem of his suit jacket and stood a tad straighter. His craggy face told her he was older than her first estimate. His face wasn't attractive, and she had to avoid fixating on the hairs growing from the mole on his chin.

"It's not extensive if you don't sell French wines."

Claire bit her tongue a fraction harder. This arrogant, suit-wearing man needed to get over himself. She wouldn't bring him down, but karma eventually would. She pasted on a smile and said, "Would you still like a drink?"

"Your best chardonnay," he replied, his voice pompous even as his top lip curled.

Patience, Claire. He's a paying customer. "Yes, sir," Claire said and served him the first chardonnay to hand. "That will be nine dollars."

The man grumbled under his breath about expensive wine, and Claire fought the urge to inform him he would've paid a lot more for a glass of imported French chardonnay. She gave the man change and watched him limp over to a table near the door.

Valerie hustled inside with her hands full of empty glasses but slowed when she spotted the man. Claire frowned, Valerie's reaction striking her as weird. The man spoke to her in a low voice. Valerie nodded and hurried over to Claire to set down the glasses.

"Do you know that man?"

"What?" Valerie's expression appeared startled. "No, he asked me a question about meals. He wanted meat stew. I told him that wasn't on the menu."

"All right. Take him a menu and let him peruse it. He's a strange one."

"You're telling me," Valerie said with distaste.

Claire served two customers and took a meal order while Valerie delivered the menu to the salesman. While Claire wiped the bar clean of beer stains, the man continued to scan the menu and pepper Valerie with questions. It was easy to tell her employee was becoming increasingly uncomfortable. Claire monitored the pair, even as she prayed that the man didn't start making a habit of stopping in during his travels. He handed back the menu, and Valerie nodded. She took two steps before the man called her back. It looked as if he'd asked another question.

After a brief nod, Valerie beelined to the bar. "He wants the blue cod, chips, and salad, and," she said, drawing out the word, "he wants a room for two nights."

It was clear from her tone that Valerie hadn't taken to the man either. Claire considered rejecting the man's request, but she was barely scraping by and needed the patronage. "Tell him... No, don't worry. I'll pass the order to the kitchen, then speak to him myself."

"Thanks." The word sounded heartfelt.

Claire wandered over a few minutes later. "I understand you'd like a room."

"For two nights," the man said.

"Mister....?"

"Mr. Mercer," the man said, slightly twisting his lips in what Claire thought was a smile. It didn't come close.

"Mr. Mercer, I have a room available tonight but not tomorrow. We're fully booked this weekend. If you don't want to shift accommodations, it might be best if you book elsewhere. I can show you the room if that will help."

"No, you're right. It would be much easier if I didn't have to unpack and repack my belongings. Do you have any suggestions?"

"The Manchester, on the lakefront, might work. If you like, I can call them for you. The views are gorgeous, and the rooms are top-notch since the management refurbished them last year."

"No, that's all right. I'll have lunch and walk afterward to help settle my meal. Just down the road, you say?"

"Yes."

Mr. Mercer abruptly nodded and shunted his empty glass toward her, his hand surprisingly delicate with long, pale fingers. "More wine."

As Claire took the glass, an insect buzzed past her head. "Ugh." She slapped her hand at the fly and missed.

Before Claire could blink, Mr. Mercer's hand whipped out, and he closed his hands around the fly. "I don't like to see any living creature die. I'll put the insect outside and wash my hands before I eat. Which way are the restrooms?"

"Out the door over there and to the right," Claire replied, pointing to illustrate her words. What a peculiar man. Given the opportunity, who didn't want to squish a fly?

The man stalked off without a word of gratitude. Thankfully, most of her customers were considerably more polite than Mr. Mercer.

Claire returned to the bar and sent Valerie on a break. The girl grabbed a glass of water and headed outside to get fresh air while Claire settled back into her routine of serving customers. The bodies in the pub had thinned out since Fergus's family had left. She wondered how long they'd stay since they were excellent for business.

The strange Mr. Mercer returned, and Claire delivered his meal and another glass of wine. It was only when she was halfway back to the bar that she had a strange thought. The man's hands. They didn't fit with his craggy face since they'd been unblemished and elegant. Perhaps he was a musician? Shrugging, she positioned herself behind the bar and served the next customer. She'd save her brainpower for her polite patrons who didn't treat her like a convenience.

The door opened, and a man entered. Claire handed over a beer and took the money for the drink. The door banged again.

"Holy cow!" a loud voice shouted.

"Watch out!" a second cried as a chair crashed to the floor, and general panic filled the outdoor area.

Claire set down the glass she'd picked up to fill with orange juice.

"Watch the bar," she snapped at her part-timer. She raced outside with many of her customers to witness a black dragon take off with Iain's brother and Valerie. The dragon flung itself upward, wings beating strongly while Valerie shrieked. Her panicked cries rippled through the air, but neither the dragon nor the man holding her paid the slightest notice. The dragon swiftly flew over the mountain and vanished from sight.

Were they abducting her?

"What happened? Did anyone see?" Claire asked, a jittery sensation in the pit of her stomach. Valerie hadn't gone willingly. She'd screamed.

An elderly man snorted. "Stupid question. The kid morphed into a dragon and flew off."

Claire strove for patience, digging her hands into her jeans pockets to hide her balled fingers. "What happened before that? Before the man became a dragon?"

"Weren't more than a kid," the elderly man retorted.

Claire cleared her throat, and when that didn't prompt a satisfactory explanation, she turned to a group of five women who'd been having lunch before returning to work. "Did you see or hear what happened?"

A tall blonde frowned. "I'm uncertain because we weren't paying attention, but I noticed your barmaid sat with them during her break. They were talking in low voices, and once, when I glanced in their direction, I thought they were arguing, but then I saw her kissing one." She shook her head, and another woman took up the story.

The short brunette wearing a tight black skirt teamed with a white and black pinstriped blouse and black shoes with towering heels pursed her lips. "I saw her kiss both guys. They weren't friendly pecks. It was more like the kisses of a lover."

Claire scowled, glancing at the silhouettes of mountains

and the vast blue sky. "You think she went willingly?"

"That's what was weird," the brunette said, pursing her lips again. "She giggled, flirted even, until the man—not the dragon—picked her up. He slapped her over the buttocks, and that's when she started to scream and struggle. She knocked over the chair with her flailing."

"I see. Thank you for your help." Claire marched back into the bar, anger pulsing through her. How dare Fergus's relations kidnap her bar staff? The second her next worker arrived, she intended to confront Fergus and demand Valerie's return.

6

FERGUS AND IAIN SAT in his minuscule office and studied the results of Nikau's autopsy. The vet had found nothing new during his careful examination of Sam's wolf.

Fergus tapped his fingers on his desktop. "The lack of leads is frustrating the hell out of me."

Iain leaned back in his chair, making it creak alarmingly before he resettled with a thump. He counted, using his fingers. "One, you have hairs of unknown origin. Two, there's the unusual scent, which could be a paranormal creature or unrelated. And three, the purple flies."

"All dead ends," Fergus said. "Where do we go next?"

The outer door to the station flung open with a resounding whack when it hit the stopper. Fergus straightened to attention, and Iain cocked his head, his muscles coiling in preparation.

"Fergus Murray!" a furious feminine voice shouted.

Fergus glanced at Iain, and his brother-in-law relaxed.

"You done something to piss off Claire?" Humor lurked in Iain despite the dry note in his voice.

"Not that I know of," Fergus said, rising. He exited his office and walked into the reception area with two single chairs and several posters regarding police services and safety messages decorating the wall.

Claire stood at the reception counter, her hands clenched at her sides. Temper had colored her face a delicate pink, and he couldn't help but stare. She had never looked so gorgeous and sexy. So delectable he had to forcibly halt his urge to gather her into his arms.

"Do something about your family," she snapped.

Fergus's stomach dropped, and caution sprang to the fore. "Why? What's happened?"

Iain pushed his way past Fergus for a clear view of Claire. "Something wrong?"

"I don't know where they come in your family relationships, but those two young men kidnapped my employee. She screamed in terror until the dragon vanished over the mountain." Claire glowered at him and aimed an equally dark glare Iain's way. "They abducted her."

That didn't sound right. Fergus rounded the counter and shunted a trembling Claire toward one of the visitor chairs. "What happened?"

"Didn't you listen?" Her voice rose to a shriek, and he winced.

"Tell me again. Start at the beginning."

Fergus listened closely to everything Claire told him. The reluctance to take a break. The clatter of garden furniture outside. On investigation, she'd seen a black dragon flying off with two human figures. Claire described everything she'd seen and learned from witnesses, finishing with, "Fergus, find them. She's a young girl. She didn't ask for this, and you must remove her from the situation as soon as possible."

Fergus exchanged a puzzled glance with Iain, who seemed as shocked as he. Their brothers didn't go around kidnapping women. "Claire, we want to live harmoniously with humans. We would never bring attention to ourselves by abducting a human woman. I'm sure there is an explanation."

Claire lifted her chin. "Valerie was screaming."

Fergus exchanged a helpless look with Iain. He didn't believe Finn and James had kidnapped Valerie.

"Times have changed," Claire said, sounding frustrated. "Now paranormals don't have to worry about repercussions."

"Not true," Fergus said instantly. He wanted to embrace her until she stopped shaking. He longed for her comforting touch, remembering how she felt in his arms. "Do you believe that? The law applies to us the same way. Along with human laws, we have rules our leaders enforce."

"Enough!" Claire snapped, slashing her right hand through the air. "I don't care. You need to recover Valerie before she's traumatized for life. A woman should be able to flirt with a guy without him misunderstanding."

"You're right. What direction did they go?"

"I told you. Across the lake and up over the mountains."

"Come outside. Show us," Fergus said, aiming for calm and in control when his insides jangled insistently like a pinball machine in the hands of an expert. Except this was no game. What the hell was happening in his town? A murder and now this. Although his family was involved, and they'd always been unpredictable. But not unlawful. Never criminals.

"Fergus!"

The sharp note in Claire's voice had him blinking. He hadn't heard that from her before, and she piqued his interest. He'd already liked and admired her and craved a repeat of their night in Queenstown. Until now, he'd kept his distance, but...

"There were dozens of witnesses. Fergus, what's wrong with you? Do something. Get a search party. Rescue that poor girl."

"A search party won't be necessary," Fergus said. "You told me it was my nephew and my brother. Iain and I will find them and bring Valerie back."

"Take me with you," Claire said, lifting her chin as if she expected him to argue.

Damn right. He'd shut this down before she took over the entire investigation. "No."

Claire grasped his arm, her glare dark and stormy. "Valerie will need comfort."

"No," Fergus repeated. Didn't she understand he'd have to fly? There was no other way to track them.

Iain pulled out his phone, and Fergus heard his dad's gruff hello. "Dougal, are Finn and James there?"

"No, they went to the pub for a drink before going out

on the lake. They've met some locals who invited them fishing."

Relief swept through Fergus. Claire was mistaken.

"They were going fishing," Fergus said for Claire's benefit.

She tapped on his chest, an impatient drumming of fingers. "Ask him about Valerie."

"Dad, were they intending to meet Valerie?"

"Possibly. They both have a crush on her and were arguing about who would ask her out."

Fergus groaned, instinct telling him now that what Claire had witnessed wasn't a figment of her imagination. A glance at Iain told him his brother-in-law suspected Claire might not be exaggerating either.

"What's wrong?" his father asked. "Something I can help with?"

"Claire informed us Finn and James abducted Valerie. They flew into the mountains, with Valerie screaming," Iain said.

"Are you certain?" his father asked, sounding as shocked as Fergus.

"I'm afraid so," Iain said. "Claire says dozens of her customers witnessed the abduction."

"Crap," his father said.

A hell of an understatement. "Do you know where they might go?" Fergus spoke, knowing his father would hear without difficulty.

"James took Finn flying yesterday. From what they told your mother, they flew into the mountains and explored on foot."

"Right. Dad, get them to contact me when they arrive home. Iain and I will search for them in the meantime."

"Is Elspeth busy?" Iain asked.

"She's playing outside with the boys. I'll watch the kids. I'll get her to meet you—where are you?"

"At the police station," Iain said. "Thanks, Dougal." He disconnected the call.

"We'll leave now," Fergus said. "I'm sure we'll find Valerie unharmed."

"Didn't you hear? I'm coming with you." Round spots of pink stood out on the apple of her cheeks.

"And if I refuse to take you?"

Pure temper flashed in her then, and Fergus wondered if something was wrong with him because he was enjoying this feisty side of her.

Claire's features tightened, and a vein pulsed and twitched at her temple. Her beautiful eyes flashed. "Stop mucking around, Fergus Murray. Time is wasting."

Iain shot him a smirk and strode for the front door. "Elspeth and I will wait for you."

Fergus read his thoughts as easily as if Iain had spoken them aloud. He was doomed.

Fergus gave in as he'd known he would on hearing Claire's suggestion, the temptation of showing off his dragon form too great. He followed her outside. "You'll need warm clothes and hiking boots."

"I'll run home and get changed."

"Pack a daypack with first aid supplies, water, and, if possible, a couple of chocolate or energy bars," Fergus instructed. "I'll arrive shortly."

Claire turned to leave before halting and turning back to him with a scowl. "You'd better not leave without me, Fergus Murray. That would piss me off."

Fergus bit back his grin. The idea had crossed his mind.

"I won't do that," he said simply once he had a handle on his inappropriate burst of humor. "Five minutes. Don't keep me waiting."

Her flash of irritation amused him, and he had the weird impulse to take her in his arms and kiss the furrow between her brows before she stomped away. He ogled her attractive backside until something struck his head.

He whirled in time to see a young man launch a missile at him. An egg. It smashed harmlessly on the ground beside him. His nose twitched at the reek. *A rotten egg.* Fergus dodged the next object, fired by the man's friend. A third person—a woman raised her arm to throw.

"Enough," he roared. "Cease immediately, or I'll arrest you for assault of a police officer."

"We're not listening to no dragon punk," the woman retorted, her round face twisted into a sneer.

"Yeah, you need to leave. We don't want you here," one man said.

"This is a human town!" the second man yelled.

"Whatever," Fergus said and re-entered the police station. He plucked his phone off his desk and stuffed it in his pocket. What else did he need? He ran through a mental checklist and grabbed his small portable first aid kit before locking his community station and turning the sign to closed.

To his relief, the egg-wielders had left, the stinky yellow

smears the only evidence of their presence. He turned toward Claire's residence, his long strides eating up the distance. She was sitting on her front stoop and pulling on a pair of worn-in hiking boots as he arrived.

"Are you ready? We need to meet Iain and Elspeth back at the police station. I'll give you my phone and my first aid supplies. You'll need to carry them for me."

Her gaze lifted, full of questions. Her throat worked in a swallow. Ah! She wasn't as brave as she'd made out. "Um. Okay."

Fergus took a step back and stooped to remove his boots and socks. Next, he removed his shirt. Claire gaped at him, watching the entire process, her eyes growing wider and wider with each piece of discarded uniform.

"W-what are you doing?" she demanded, close to a screech.

Fergus chuckled, enjoying this ruffled side of her. "If I shift to dragon now, I'll destroy my uniform."

"You'll be naked?"

"You've seen me naked before."

She spluttered, and he barked out a laugh, his amusement echoing in Claire's tiny porch.

Claire glared at him. "This isn't funny. You're not taking Valerie's abduction seriously. She's my best worker and slots in with my team so well. You didn't hear her scream, her terror."

Fergus stepped out of his trousers and thrust them at her. "Please pack my trousers and my socks. If my boots won't fit, tie them to the outside of my pack. *Do not* drop them because they were expensive."

"Don't you want your shirt?"

"The cold doesn't bother me. I'll leave that here with the other unnecessary stuff."

While Claire busied herself following his instructions, Fergus stepped out of his boxer-briefs and folded them inside his shirt. He tucked them in a sheltered spot under an old white rocking chair to his right.

"Claire."

Claire glanced at him, her gaze giving him a quick up and down before settling on his face. A blush climbed into her cheeks, but he didn't tease her.

"This is important. Once I shift, we won't be able to communicate. I'll kneel as much as I can. You'll need to sit on my shoulders and hang on tight. I'll try not to do deep dives or sudden moves, but don't let go until we land. Can you do that?"

"Yes." Her gaze dropped to his chest. It seemed without volition, yet it took her long seconds to notice her lapse.

He cleared his throat, and she released a gasp, the pink in her cheeks deepening to a rosy hue.

"Sorry," she muttered and shrugged the pack onto her shoulders.

Aware of the passing time, Fergus quit with his teasing and stepped back to leave himself plenty of room to shift. He centered his mind and drew a mental picture of his sooty-black dragon before letting the transformation slide over him. He never heard the sounds or felt the reforming bones that someone witnessing him morph might hear.

Instead, there was euphoria in embracing everything he could be. His sight intensified. His sense of smell improved tenfold, and despite his tough black scales, he was aware of every shift of the wind.

He turned his head, now at the end of a longer neck, to observe Claire's reaction. Dealing with humans was always challenging, and their responses were unpredictable. Claire gaped at him with her big, dark blue eyes. They held wonder and awe instead of the fear he'd worried he might face.

Fergus kneeled, and she eyed him dubiously. She was average height and would never be skinny with her decided curves, while he was huge in his dragon form.

Claire wrinkled her nose. "I'll get my stepstool." She hustled away, and Fergus permitted himself to stare at the spectacular view. He loved a curvy arse on a woman, and Claire had a fantastic one.

She reappeared a few minutes later, dragging her stepstool, her pace hurried. Words of caution rushed to Fergus's mind. She shouldn't rush. He doubted Valerie was in danger from his brother or Finn. The pair were sensible and would never risk injuring a human.

Both knew better.

Like most dragons and other supernatural creatures, they'd had safety and the necessity to temper their strength drummed into them since they were youngsters. Neither had caused a kerfuffle in the past, and Fergus doubted their arrival in Te Anau had changed them, despite Claire's assertions.

Jerked from his thoughts, he waited for Claire to arrange her step before he sidled up to it and kneeled again.

"Perfect," Claire said, sounding breathless as she

clambered onto his back.

She wrapped her legs around him as best she could. "I've ridden horses since I was a teenager," she said. "I'm sure that this won't be much different.

Except he wasn't a horse.

Fergus waited until she gripped the jagged spike in front of her. Despite the uncomfortable seating arrangement between spikes, they would travel quickly and search on foot at the mountaintop. The boys wouldn't have traveled far—not with a screaming Valerie.

He lifted into the air with a mighty flap of his wings, smirking when Claire gave a little shriek and increased her grip. This had to be a misunderstanding. He didn't believe James or Finn would become involved in a kidnapping. Despite his crazy family, they wouldn't draw attention or cause trouble for him.

7

CLAIRE SANK HER TEETH into her bottom lip to block her panicked scream. She was only partially successful.

Holy Hannah! What had she been thinking?

Demanding to go along on the search? Ludicrous.

She hadn't thought through the details. And now, due to her stupidity, she sat astride a soaring dragon. A magnificent dragon. Yep, but the ground was miles below. It would hurt if she fell.

At that thought, a strangled laugh emerged, the high, almost hysterical sound immediately blown away by the wind.

This was Fergus.

She was riding Fergus. That overwrought laugh rose a notch to a level near crazed. Not words she'd dared to think, let alone admit. The man she lusted after, the one she'd slept with in Queenstown, was a freakin' massive dragon. His muscles bunched beneath her trembling thighs, and his giant black wings flapped. He soared past the police station with surprising speed and agility, and Claire shrieked when he swooped toward the mountains, coming frighteningly close to a tree. He veered away, turning his giant head to look at her. His golden gaze held remonstration, and her breath caught, cutting off her scream. The abrupt silence didn't still her agitated mind.

She hadn't considered the details. The repercussions. All she'd wanted was to help Valerie. Abducting women was unacceptable. She hadn't considered how she'd travel with Fergus to hunt for Valerie—the logistics. And she certainly hadn't imagined she'd see the man buck naked.

A vision of his long legs, muscled thighs, his broad shoulders, and his smug grin flickered behind her closed eyes like an erotic movie. She'd tried not to stare like a peeper. She really had, but her gaze had darted to him without volition, and she'd been able to appreciate *all* of him in his naked splendor—more than she'd seen during the night they'd spent together. The wretched man had known it, too. Even his dragon form was sexy with his gleaming black scales.

And she was at his mercy.

Her hands tightened on the spike before her, and her thigh muscles clenched. This wasn't exactly comfortable. She stared ahead at the mountains and tried to focus on the scenery. The jagged peaks of stone. The mysteriously deep lake. Toppling off Fergus's back and striking either would undoubtedly kill her outright. She swallowed hard and concentrated on remaining in place. It wasn't easy, given her uncomfortable position. She only hoped she could walk straight once they landed because dragon chafe was a thing.

A black dragon glided in the distance, carrying a man. Elspeth and Iain. Her mind slid back to her current predicament.

She'd thought Fergus would've fought harder about taking her along. Now that they were aloft, she realized how vulnerable she was alone with him, the other dragon, and a wolf. She'd known him for months. She kept reminding herself of that. He worked hard and was a decent guy.

Since he'd come out as a dragon, Claire had noticed people giving him the side-eye. She'd heard whispers, and there had been a bit of nastiness. She actively ignored gossip while working the bar.

Now, she'd put herself in the position of protecting one of her staff. She groaned inwardly, a huge part of her acknowledging she shouldn't have allowed her temper to hold sway.

The air whipped through her hair, yanking strands from her ponytail. She shivered, the frigid breeze seeping through her open jacket. If she weren't terrified of falling, she'd release her grip on Fergus's spike and try to do up her jacket zipper.

Fergus reached the height of the mountain range, and the alpine vista sprawled before her—tussock grasses and stubby bushes and the Luxmore hut with the slopes of Mount Luxmore looming behind. A group of three trampers making their way along the track to reach the hut ceased walking and stared at the dragons. Then, she didn't notice their gawking audience because she was struggling to remain upright with the drag of the wind roaring over the ridge. Fear lurched through her stomach as she lost her grip. The insides of her legs felt raw even though she'd worn hiking pants.

A scream rippled from her throat, swiftly carried away by the prevailing wind. Fergus continued flying steadily toward the hut, and to her relief, he landed on the helicopter pad.

Several hikers had already stopped for the day and relaxed on the sunny deck. They gaped until Claire felt like a bug under a microscope.

Fergus kneeled, and Claire immediately slid to the ground. Her legs shook, and her knees buckled. For an instant, she wondered if her shaky limbs would hold her, and she had the absurd notion of kissing the ground in relief. Once she'd steadied herself with the help of Fergus's scaly shoulder, she turned to him in askance.

"Why are we stopping here?"

Fergus stepped away and shifted to his human form. The transformation took moments. One second, she gaped at a dragon; the next, a splendidly naked Fergus stood before her.

"Please hand me my clothes, and I'll explain as I dress."

Good idea. Not only was it cold up here, but she didn't trust herself not to sneak another peek. The temptation... Yep, she appreciated a sexy man as much as the next.

With shaking fingers, she opened her pack and thrust Fergus's trousers at him.

"I thought we'd ask the warden and perhaps the

trampers who have reached the hut today if they've seen another dragon. If they can't help us, we'll fly to the next hut."

"What if no one has seen them?"

"We'll have to wait until they decide to return to town." Fergus pulled on his socks and boots but didn't bother about a shirt.

The other dragon flew closer and hovered.

"Scan the area," Fergus shouted. "We're checking in with the warden."

The dragon sped away, and when Claire angled back toward Fergus, she got an eye full of a broad chest. Claire took two rapid steps back. Too much temptation. She might do something foolish like touching him, and his rejection would hurt. She'd given Fergus plenty of chances to advance their relationship. Other than grabbing his hands and placing one on her butt and the other on a breast, she couldn't signal her intentions more clearly.

He seemed adamant they'd never be together romantically and had placed her firmly in the friend zone.

It hurt like a stubbed toe or a dragon-chafed thigh. He believed she wasn't good enough.

"What's wrong?" he asked when she scowled.

"Where is your shirt?"

"You know I didn't bother packing one. It's extra weight."

There was a brief pause before she said, "I'll ask those people over there." Without waiting for a reply, she left, using long strides to place distance between her and temptation. Her fingertips still tingled with the urge to

99

touch and explore those smooth muscles of his again. A shudder ran through her at the idea of gliding her palms over his bulging pectoral muscles.

Footsteps had her flashing a glance over her shoulder. Fergus marched behind her. "What are you doing?" she asked.

"I want to speak with the hut warden. She's standing in the doorway, speaking with two guests."

"Oh," Claire said in a small voice. "You should've brought a shirt. Everyone is staring."

"You're the worst offender." And with that, the wretched dragon man strode past her, a whistled tune floating in his wake.

Heat flamed her cheeks, but she still found her gaze drawn to his muscular butt, the flex of his legs in those uniform pants of his. She sighed. What a glorious sight. One day, an intelligent woman would snap him up, leaving Claire mourning lost opportunities.

With another sigh, she turned to question the group of female hikers, staring with rapt attention at Fergus and the hut caretaker.

"He's the local cop," a woman much younger than Claire said. "How much do you bet I can get into his bed before we leave town?"

The black-haired woman sitting next to her laughed softly. "That man is devoted to his job, cuz. Believe me. I, and lots of the single women in Te Anau, have tried. I doubt you'll be any more successful than us."

She wouldn't if Claire had her way.

While speaking with the hut caretaker, Fergus watched Claire. She was chatting with a group of women. Satisfaction settled on his shoulders because while she'd screamed at first, she was functioning normally now. Even better, she couldn't stop ogling him despite his dragon status. She could gawk at him anytime. Better, his family hadn't perturbed her, and she seemed to enjoy spending time with them.

Maybe he risked it and asked Claire for dinner or a picnic when she had free time. He could fly them somewhere in the Fiordland National Park and find a remote, romantic spot with guaranteed privacy. He could...

A sharp poke in his chest had him snapping his attention back to Lois Winston, the caretaker on duty at Luxmore Hut. "What did you do that for?"

"It's about time you and the beautiful Claire stopped circling each other and got together." A grinning and unrepentant Lois faced him, her salt-and-pepper hair scraped back in a ponytail. Frizzy bits had sprung free, giving her a windblown look. "And you—keeping secrets. Lucky for you, Claire doesn't seem to mind that you're a dragon. The locals will be fine once they get over the initial shock. Now, are you gonna tell me why you made such a dramatic arrival, or are you gonna keep staring at the girl's butt?"

Fergus had long mastered his expression but suspected the blunt Lois might have done the impossible and caused him to blush. "Did you see another dragon fly over around an hour ago?"

"No, but I've been head down cleaning the dormitories and toilets. Those girls arrived about two hours ago. If anyone saw anything, it'd be them. Go over and join Claire. Bet you ten dollars they'll all flutter their lashes. If you're lucky, they might proposition you." Laugh lines collected over a lifetime deepened to creases, and her shrewd blue eyes twinkled at his expense.

Fergus scowled. "Not interested." He stalked away from the elderly woman to question the other guests. Lois's mocking laughter trailed him like a puppy.

He started with the nearest group, which consisted of a man in his twenties and two women of a similar age. "Did you see a dragon fly over on your walk here?"

"We did," the guy said, his head tilting in interest. "Was that you?"

"No," Fergus replied. "Which direction are you walking?"

"We came from Iris Burn Hut today," one woman—a brunette with severely short hair—said. "We spotted the dragon around an hour and a half ago."

"Was the dragon alone?"

Frowning, the man tilted his head to shield his eyes from the sun. "I think he had two people astride him, but he flew fast and disappeared before my mind told me what I was seeing."

Fergus nodded. "Which direction did they go? Along the Kepler Track?"

"They went toward the area where they rediscovered

those birds. The takahe," the other woman said. She had long, straight brown hair cut in severe angles. "As Craig said, we didn't see them for long. They flew over the next mountain range and deeper into Fiordland National Park. We didn't even have time to take photos. Not one of my family will believe me when I tell them we saw a dragon. Our area doesn't have paranormal creatures."

"Not all feel safe enough to expose themselves to humans," Fergus said.

"I get that," the man said. "Some of the behavior has been despicable. It makes me ashamed. Should we be concerned? Is he dangerous?"

"No, he's not a risk," Fergus said. "Thanks for your time." With a polite smile, he headed toward Claire. His heart squeezed when she turned to beam at him.

"These ladies saw the dragon fly overhead. They told me he wasn't flying very high but soaring at speed."

"He flew that way," a beautiful blonde with tanned skin, blue eyes, and a predatory expression said, pointing.

Fergus closed the remaining distance between him and Claire. He hesitated for a beat longer before curving his arm around her waist. She tensed before releasing her taut muscles and leaning into him. Fergus did his level best not to cheer aloud, but his inner dragon pounded his chest and yahooed. He might have a chance with Claire. She wasn't behaving like Miranda, so he should ask her on a date.

Claire may not envision a future with a dragon, but he could be Mr. Right Now. He could live with that. Maybe.

"Thank you," Claire said when Fergus remained silent.

"Any time," the blonde said in a sultry come-hither

tone.

Fergus ignored the silent invitation as they turned away, but he felt the weight of several stares on his backside. Funny, but the gawking didn't thrill him like Claire's regard did. This thought cheered him considerably. He needed to make a move on Claire soon or lose this opportunity.

"What next? Will we fly over that way?"

"Yes," Fergus said. "But if they've landed, the chances of spotting them are slim. Look." He risked a glance at Claire. "My brother and Iain's brother are decent young men. I doubt they'd kidnap Valerie. I know they're keen on her. My father told me. Could you have heard excited screams?"

Claire leveled her glare at him without flinching. "I know what I heard."

"Okay." Fergus didn't want to argue with Claire but still harbored doubts. His brother knew not to mess with humans. Their parents had raised them to respect all species and behave appropriately.

"What will we do next?" Claire asked.

"We'll fly over that mountain ridge, and if we don't find them, we'll have to return. The group may have doubled back to Te Anau without us spotting them."

"But what if they haven't?" Claire asked.

"We'll find Valerie. Don't worry." Fergus could tell his reassurance wasn't working. "Claire, I'm sorry, but they may be impossible to find. The National Park is extensive, with large portions inaccessible by foot. We wouldn't spot someone in the lower levels of the beech forest."

Claire bit her lip, turning it a deeper red than usual. She avoided his gaze for a long time before her shoulders slumped, and she succumbed to common sense. "You're right. I don't know what I was thinking. If a man kidnaps a woman, he doesn't hide in plain sight. He takes measures to avoid discovery."

It was Fergus's turn to bite his tongue. His brother would never abduct a woman, but nothing he said would persuade her of this. He'd have to pray that Finn and James returned to Te Anau soon.

Fergus removed the clothing and footwear he'd donned earlier and turned to Claire with his garments. She blinked, and suddenly, heat roared through his body, the blood sinking to his groin with dizzying speed. Claire's eyes widened, but to her credit, she took his clothing and shoved it into her daypack. Next, she fastened his boots to the outside of her pack.

Emboldened by her reaction, Fergus let his grin blaze free. Ms. Bryce noticed him, and her flushed cheeks suggested they were experiencing the same response. Their liking was mutual, and he knew they were compatible in bed. The caution came from his side—true—but now she knew his secret. She hadn't run screaming in the opposite direction.

"Is something wrong?"

Claire's soft voice made him realize he'd zoned out, which wasn't like him. He shook the growing lust from his mind. "Thinking," he said, not untruthfully. "We'll sweep over the mountain in the direction of the hikers' dragon sighting. If we can't see anything, we must fly back to the town."

"But—"

"My energy supply is limited. I can't keep going until we find them, and it makes little sense to fly for hours without a true plan. Also, I doubt you could stay upright for much longer. My hide is tough, and without cushioning, the insides of your thighs are probably raw."

"You're right," she conceded. "Sorry, I wasn't thinking logically. I'm worried about Valerie."

"If my brother took her," Fergus said, "she will be safe. James is reliable and steady, even if he is young. Finn, his friend, is much the same."

Fergus didn't wait for more objections. He stepped away from Claire, centered his mind, and pulled up his dragon. As always, the change slid over him with remarkable speed, and the rush of endorphins offset the pain and disorientation.

He observed Claire's fascination with satisfaction and clarity. Maybe he was hurting her by pushing her away and not taking a chance. Even if, as he suspected, this would be a temporary liaison, wasn't the fleeting joy better than the deadness he'd experienced post-Miranda? That she kept drunk calling him didn't help. She wouldn't return to him now that she'd married an Auckland A-lister. Rumors were swirling about her pregnancy in the gossip columns. Not that he read them.

Claire coughed. Crap, he'd zoned out again.

Fergus kneeled beside a knee-high boulder and waited for Claire to clamber onto his back. He lifted off once he'd felt her settle into position and grasp one of his spikes for purchase. At first, he flew slowly to ensure Claire felt securely seated, but he gradually picked up speed. The afternoon sun shone from overhead, while the faint breeze carried the scent of snow from the higher peaks and the piquant green herbal scent from the plants that clung tenuously to the mountain slopes. A glittering silvery ribbon of water wound between two peaks, down a valley, and spilled into Lake Te Anau.

Fergus didn't scent any dragons, not that he'd expected to with the scarcity of dragons around here and vast distances. He hadn't picked up anything when they'd landed either, but then he hadn't believed he would because witnesses had stated the dragon flew overhead rather than landed.

He swooped low over the forests, and once the tree line ended, he flew a few feet above the rocky landscape carved by wind, rain, and snow. A deer or a chamois darted across a slope, fleeing from the lurking danger above.

Not a thing appeared out of place.

Not a single hiker walked the pristine tracks. He couldn't even spot Elspeth and Iain. When his muscles became fatigued, he wheeled back toward Te Anau. Claire's thighs tightened briefly on his shoulders as if protesting his decision to turn back, but after long seconds, she relaxed again.

The trip home was faster since he flew in a direct line. He settled in front of Claire's house and ignored the group of schoolchildren who gaped, then cheered on seeing him. The instant he bent, Claire slithered off his back, stumbling at first before her knees consented to hold her weight.

Several of the children recognized her, but she shooed them back. She tugged his clothes out of her pack and placed them within easy reach before joining the five children and distracting them while he shifted. Fergus pulled on his clothes and retrieved his phone from the zipped pocket of his jeans. He called his mother, but there was still no reply.

Right, that was his next stop. He needed to learn if he was right about his brother and friend or if Claire was correct and they'd done something foolish.

8

CLAIRE COULDN'T HELP IT. Her gaze strayed to Fergus as he dressed. Those muscles. Her stomach fluttered as she recalled how they'd felt beneath her fingertips. Sighing, she ripped her gaze from his naked torso and concentrated on the excited questions from the kids.

"Did you ride the dragon?" a little girl asked.

"Yes," Claire said.

"Was it scary? My mummy says dragons eat people," a tow-haired boy said.

Anger pulsed in Claire at the unfairness of the comment. The boy's parent was passing on erroneous information. This sort of talk spread until it sounded true when it was total rubbish. While she was sure a dragon could inflict damage and death, Fergus had integrated with the community residents. He didn't cause trouble. Instead, he dedicated himself to protecting those under his care.

"Fergus is a well-behaved dragon, and he eats meat and vegetables the same as you," Claire said in a firm voice that brooked no contradiction.

"He eats vegetables? Like green stuff?" The kid shuddered, his appalled expression making Claire want to chuckle.

Masculine laughter from behind her had Claire's lips quirking. This laughter of Fergus's was new, and she promised herself that she'd try to make him laugh more often.

Fergus stepped up beside her. "My favorite is broccoli with cheese sauce." He studied her for long seconds, his demeanor becoming workmanlike. "I have police business."

The kids continued to loiter. Yeah, not the time to ask probing questions with small ears around. They'd repeat everything to their friends and parents when information was better contained. "I'll be at the pub," she said. "Thanks for humoring me."

"Let me know if Valerie turns up. I'll drop by later this evening." Fergus leaned closer to tweak her nose. "You can ask your questions then."

"Thank you." Claire hesitated, then stood on tiptoes and kissed Fergus's cheek. She kissed and ran, part of her embarrassed by the impulse and part not wanting to witness Fergus's reaction. Coward, she chided herself as she limped toward her front door. Before returning to the pub, she needed a shower to ease her aching muscles.

Now that they'd returned, doubts crept into her mind. Valerie had screamed, but what if Fergus was right, and it was a lark for the three youngsters? She'd screamed during part of her flight with Fergus.

Claire pushed open her front door and stepped inside her sun-dappled entrance. Every muscle in her arms and shoulders ached, and she suspected if she lined up with a group of cowboys, her bowed legs wouldn't look out of place.

The kauri floorboards creaked as she hobbled down the passage to her bathroom. She stared longingly at the tub beneath a stained-glass window for a moment. No time. She sighed and disrobed.

"Ouch," she muttered. "I sat on my arse the entire time. Why do I hurt so much?"

The shower's heat helped, and she wasn't limping as severely when she entered the pub. One visual sweep told her the customers seemed contented with their lot. Luckily, one of her reliable and long-term part-timers had come in to help since she typically couldn't go off on a jaunt like she had this afternoon.

The instant her thoughts veered in his direction, she called up a vision of him sans clothes. Muscles. Strength. Sexiness.

All attractive qualities in a man.

A dragon.

Claire groaned and went to check on the kitchen and her cook. How was she going to handle Fergus? Until this afternoon, she'd thought he wasn't interested, but now...

Had she imagined that flash of heat in his eyes?

"Could've been a dragon thing," she muttered. "Who knows?"

"Pardon?" Her cook paused in the plating of a cheeseburger. "Did you say something?"

"Talking to myself," Claire said with a smile.

The elderly lady grinned, baring a missing front tooth. "Too right. The best way to get the perfect answer." With the burger done, she carried it to the serving hatch and thumped the bell that signaled a completed order.

Claire wrinkled her nose. "Any problems?"

The lady tapped her wooden spoon against the side of her pot. A dull ring competed with the oven timer. "Not a one. Everyone is too busy gossiping about that sexy man of yours."

"He's not mine," Claire protested.

The cook reached to turn off the timer and ambled to the oven. "He could be if you got your arse into gear. I've seen how he devours you when he thinks no one will notice."

"N-no," Claire stuttered. "No, you're wrong."

"And I've seen the goo-goo eyes you make back."

Claire clamped her mouth shut and decided on a strategic retreat. The woman's delighted cackle followed Claire to the bar.

When Fergus retrieved his phone, the screen lit up with messages and missed calls. He scanned them, pleased to have a chore to take his mind off Claire. As soon as her name popped into his mind, his cheek tingled right where she'd kissed him. He recalled her delectable floral scent.

Nothing too strong but the delicate fragrance of spring flowers. Despite their audience of curious kids, every part of him had wanted to kiss her properly.

Thankfully, shock had frozen him, and in those precious seconds, she'd danced away and hightailed it to her cottage.

He read a message from Iain. *Need to talk. Urgent.* Fergus frowned. Had they found James and Finn? Before contacting them, he listened to his voicemail in case Iain or Elspeth had left a message.

Miranda's voice was a kick in the gut. "Fergus, why don't you ever return your messages? I'm so unhappy with Jared. I've made a huge mistake. Please, take me back."

Fergus let the message move to the next one in the queue.

Miranda's voice poured into his ears again. "Fergus, it's you I love. I was so stupid and shouldn't have listened to my parents. I should've trusted my gut and stayed with you."

Fergus growled. Five months ago, a call like this would've delighted him. Her drunken slur came in a third message, her words less decipherable with each call.

"I'm pregnant, Fergus. Please call me and let me come home."

Fergus deleted each of her calls and the six others she'd made without listening to them. Based on experience, he anticipated more of the same. The baby wasn't his because in the last three months they'd been together, she'd refused to sleep with him, citing fear of him losing control.

The entire debacle had started when the government

passed new laws regarding paranormal creatures. A few days later, he'd told her of his dragon status and asked her to marry him.

Yeah, that had gone well.

Claire slipped into his mind, and the tension in his shoulders released. Claire was utterly different from Miranda. The pub owner achieved success independently, without relying on a man. Her self-sufficiency attracted him more than Miranda's stunning beauty. Miranda possessed a temper, and things had become plain ugly whenever she'd lost her grip on her anger. He couldn't see Claire behaving in that manner.

He grinned. Yeah, she'd spoken sharply today, ordering him around, but she'd used her words. His dragon heritage hadn't been a problem. Claire showed concern for others—her friends and customers, a direct contrast with Miranda, who always focused on her needs.

He knew which woman he preferred to stand at his side. If only he had the guts to ask Claire out.

His phone rang. His brother-in-law.

"Iain, what's up?"

"You know the foreign scent I identified at your place? The one we couldn't identify?"

Fergus straightened. "Yeah."

"I picked it up again when I walked along the lakefront. It disappeared at a hotel, but I didn't go inside. Thought I should wait for you."

"Where are you now?" Fergus asked.

"We're leaving for dinner—a place on the main street. Don't know the name."

"No problem. I'll call Mum and join you there. We'll go out after dinner. I'd prefer to keep this on the down-low and not involve Mum and Dad."

"What if the person leaves the hotel?"

"Since it's evening, they're probably safely tucked away, or they will be by the time we arrive at the hotel." Fergus paused, second-guessing himself. If the person of interest remained in the hotel, they could quietly contact the owner and get information. They'd go in forearmed. "You're happy to be my backup?"

"Yes," Iain said.

"I'll call Mum and invite myself to join the family."

Iain made a scoffing sound. "While Dougal and Fiona are enjoying the scenery and meeting the locals, they're here to spend time with you."

"Right," Fergus said, knowing Iain spoke the truth. "I'll call Ma now. Wait, Finn and James. Have they turned up? Did you or Elspeth spot them?"

"We enjoyed the flight, but no dragon sighting. You?"

"Several hikers saw them, but we didn't spot them either."

"How did Claire cope?" Iain asked, his tone slipping close to teasing.

"She kissed me."

"Huh," Iain said. "Your mum will be pleased to hear that."

"Don't you dare tell her."

"See ya later," Iain said and hung up.

Fergus scowled at his phone. Bloody Iain. His mother would double down on matchmaking if she even suspected his interest in Claire.

At five minutes to six, he left his house, securing the door when he usually left his home unlocked. Minutes later, he turned the corner to find his family about to enter the restaurant.

"I'm so glad you had time to come to dinner," his mother said, hugging him. "Especially with your work commitments."

"I enjoy spending time with my family."

His mother tilted her head and straightened the collar of his plain white cotton shirt. "I thought you were ashamed of us."

Fergus shook his head. "I kept my identity secret to make my job easier, but now that you've forced me out into the open, I'm glad." The truth, although his family had unwittingly slammed any chance he had of promotion.

En mass, they entered the restaurant. His sister spoke to the hostess and organized their seating once they reached their reserved table.

"When are you going to ask out the woman that runs the pub?" his father asked while they waited for Elspeth's orders. "She likes you. I'm positive she'll say yes."

"Dad." A glance at his mother told of her frank interest, her nosiness, and he winced inwardly but continued. "Miranda brutalized my heart, and I couldn't go through that again. I want to take my time with Claire." Fergus gave his parents honesty instead of fobbing them off or telling them to butt out.

His father pulled him in for a quick hug and patted his back, his dark eyes sparkling with approval and respect.

His mother hugged him next and placed a noisy kiss on his cheek.

"The young lady wasn't right for you, but I have an excellent feeling about this one."

"Me too," Fergus said, heading for the seat Elspeth waved him toward.

It was relaxing to chill with his family, although it was difficult to ignore the nosy interest from the other customers.

His mother waved their curiosity away with her usual humor. "Next time, we'll charge a gawking fee," she said.

"Or at least ask the restaurant for a discounted meal since we've attracted extra diners," Iain quipped.

Fergus glanced over his shoulder to scan the restaurant. Iain was right. Every table was full, and the servers hustled, dodging deftly between tables, their hands full of plates of decadently scented food. Fergus shrugged and returned to his meal, but now he felt the weight of probing stares, and his appetite faded.

His father leaned over and grasped his forearm. "Don't worry, son. We're a novelty at present. No doubt the government will cause a ruckus with some new policy. They're making a hash of things as we speak."

Fergus rolled his eyes. "Tell me about it. What are you doing tomorrow?"

"We're finally taking a trip on the ship, *Faith*. They were full when we tried to book tickets earlier. They do a commentary, give you drinks and snacks, and stop near the hidden lakes. I love the old boats," his father said. "My grandfather worked on one similar in Scotland. They'd cart goods up and down the coast. I understand they built this one in Scotland, so I look forward to hearing the crew mention the boat's history. It looks in good shape."

His mother leaned closer and lowered her voice. "How is your work going?"

"Slowly. I'm frustrated with the lack of leads. How did you know?"

"Iain mentioned the murder." She frowned. "The locals don't seem bothered."

Fergus scowled, having noted that fact himself. "Do you know if James and Finn took their phones or a locator beacon?"

His mother snorted. "Why would they need a locator beacon? James has his natural dragon sense of direction in the air, and Finn has his power of scent on the land."

"Their phones?"

"I presume so," his mother said. "Young folk these days are surgically attached to their gadgets."

"True. I've tried several times but haven't contacted them yet. I got a ringtone at one stage, but the phone cut off. Probably the mountain ranges getting in the way."

"Neither Dougal nor I are concerned. They're great kids and very responsible."

"Apart from them enticing Valerie to duck out of work. Claire is short-staffed," Fergus said, an edge to his voice.

"Is she now?" his father said. "That's too bad."

"It's easy to see why you like this posting, son," his mother said. "It's quiet, and most humans have treated us with politeness. The kids love the space and freedom to run and play in either form. They had a terrific time playing with three dogs this morning at the playland. The dogs enjoyed the rough and tumble as much as the boys. Once Elspeth assured their owners that the boys wouldn't hurt their pets, it was a joyful encounter to watch. They played with the kids on the swings, although Elspeth mentioned a few parents objected to their nakedness."

Fergus grinned, finding it easy to imagine the scene.

A large group of nearby diners finished their meal and stood to leave. Fergus nodded at a couple he knew. They stopped to chat, and he introduced them to his parents. Iain stood and disappeared toward the restrooms.

"You live in a delightful town," his father said after shaking hands with the local school principal.

"We think so," the principal's wife, a tall, rail-thin brunette in a severe black suit, said. "It's lovely to meet you."

"Fergus." Iain spoke sharply, grabbing Fergus's attention. "Can I speak with you?" After spearing Fergus with a piercing glance, Iain strode to the restaurant exit, determined to keep their family from eavesdropping.

Everything inside Fergus tightened at Iain's urgency, and he followed his brother-in-law with ground-eating steps.

When he joined Iain outside, Iain started talking. "The person who left the scent at the murder scene is here. Or they've walked past our table, either going to the restrooms or leaving with the large group."

"You're sure?"

"Quick, down here." Iain slid into an alley between the restaurant and the florist next door.

Once they stood in the shadows, Iain flung off his footwear and clothes and thrust them at Fergus.

"I'll shift and pick up their trail. If they go to that hotel, we'll know that we—you—should question them."

Fergus rapidly folded Iain's clothes. "You find the trail, and I'll follow."

Iain shifted and wasted no time. Fergus trotted behind the wolf, his arms full of Iain's clothing and boots. No doubt, a comical picture. He didn't care. If this led to catching Samuel's murderer, the locals and visitors could laugh all they wanted.

Iain sniffed at the entrance to the restaurant before turning left, trotting briskly. Instead of the trail leading to the hotel as Fergus had thought it would, the scent meandered through the town's main street and stopped at a dairy. Iain continued sniffing while Fergus set the clothes and boots down and entered the twenty-four-hour shop, stocking groceries, drinks, and confectionery. The scent of meat pies heating in the warmer blasted him, along with a faint trace of BO and the lingering notes of a designer perfume.

Finding the place empty, he approached the counter to question the Indian male attendant. He'd interrupted his dinner because the man had a smudge of ketchup on one side of his mouth.

"Any customers in the last ten minutes?" Fergus asked.

"I've just taken over from my niece," the man said. "She told me business has been slow with only a few customers."

"Thanks." Fergus retraced his steps to join Iain

outdoors, shaking his head. Iain trotted in ever-widening circles and yipped when he found the scent again. Surprisingly, the trail didn't continue directly from the dairy. Fergus made a mental note to discuss this with Iain before he charged after the impatient werewolf.

9

THE SCENT MUST'VE FADED and reappeared randomly because Iain stopped and started, his sharp growl displaying frustration as he worked to pick up the trail. Three-quarters of an hour later, Iain came to a halt and snarled.

He stepped away from Fergus and shifted.

"I don't understand. The scent ebbs in and out. I've never struck this before."

"Is the man masking his scent somehow?"

"That's the only logical conclusion." Iain stepped into his jeans and tugged on a shirt. "This is a paranormal creature, but I'm unfamiliar with their species. You still can't pick up the scent?"

"No." Fergus rubbed the back of his neck, a twitchy sensation urging him to pace. "My sense of smell rarely deserts me like this."

"What about your parents? Or Elspeth?"

"I don't like to involve them. Besides, if I can't pinpoint the trail, chances are they won't either."

"What will you do?"

"I don't know. For all we know, the culprit isn't staying at the hotel. They're wily enough to commit a murder in broad daylight with no one hearing or seeing a thing. They could be playing us if they can manipulate their scent."

"Thought had crossed my mind," Iain agreed. "I'll run in the morning and try to detect the scent."

"Be careful," Fergus warned. "Make sure Mum and Dad know you're running. Send me a text."

"Will do. How about I turn on the locator on my phone? I normally keep it off since I can sniff out my phone if I mislay it."

"Great idea. Encourage the rest of the family to follow suit."

"They'll ask questions," Iain warned.

"Refer them to me. I'm heading to the pub. I'll buy you a drink."

Iain's phone buzzed, and he checked the incoming message. "Elspeth. She's wondering what's going on. Maybe tomorrow. I like to keep my wife happy."

Fergus took a deep breath. "I'm going to see Claire. I intend to ask her out to dinner. Some sort of outing."

Iain clapped him over the back. "About time. I like her. She's more accepting than many humans. Most down here aren't openly hostile. It's not the same in Auckland."

Fergus studied his brother-in-law, his impassive expression, and frowned. "Has it been that bad?"

Iain hesitated as if he were choosing his words carefully.

"Bad enough that we decided we'd take a holiday. I hope things have settled down by the time we return home."

"And if they haven't?"

Iain shrugged one shoulder. "Your parents, Elspeth, and I discussed this. We'll move to keep the kids safe. We can protect ourselves, but the boys are vulnerable."

Fergus shook his head, denying the possibility even as his chest grew tight. "I hadn't realized things were that bad. I mean, I hesitated to make my paranormal blood known, but that's because of police politics." He pulled a face, and Iain laughed.

"You wouldn't have if we hadn't outed you."

"Correct," Fergus said. "So far, the fallout hasn't been too troublesome. A few idiots, but nothing I can't deal with. We'll see what happens in the next few months."

"Good luck with Claire." Iain raised a hand in farewell and headed home.

Fergus watched his brother-in-law lope away in the human version of his werewolf strides. He hated knowing a human would pick on his nephews because they were different.

They were rambunctious—sure—but they were also intelligent and understood they had to temper their strength when they played with their classmates. As far as he knew, neither of the children had ever slipped in their careful behavior. For his sister and Iain to drag them out of school meant things were tense.

Dang, they were kids and shouldn't need to deal with adult pettiness. Fergus turned toward the pub, eagerness fueling his pace. He hurried through the back streets and alleys, his mind occupied by his nephews. He'd question his parents the next time he saw them.

The pandemic had changed everything with the millions of deaths throughout the world. Luckily, the tricky virus hadn't spread among the paranormal species, and with the paranormal scientists' help, humans had manufactured a vaccine to slow the spread.

Humans quickly forgot the unselfish aid, and some were now reluctant to embrace those who were different. He'd bet that the nastiness passed from parents to their children, who then picked on or teased the paranormal kids. This sort of thing hadn't happened in Te Anau.

Yet.

Fergus silently vowed he'd stomp out any shenanigans of this nature before they gained force. No one, paranormal, human, homeless, or elderly, should need to have their circumstances worsened because of ignorance.

He stilled when he caught a wisp of scent, much like what Iain had described earlier. It was wild and tangy, almost gamey and similar to that he'd noted briefly in his garden. Before he could determine the direction, the breeze swirled and whisked it away. He whispered a soft curse as he rotated, trying to locate the source.

Nothing jumped out at him.

Somehow, the owner was disguising his odor, or hell, perhaps he and Iain were snatching at air, imagining trouble when this was unrelated.

Fergus turned onto the street where the pub sat smack in the middle of several other buildings. Three young men left the pub, trailed by two chattering girls and a stooped man in a long coat. He tested their scents out of habit, but nothing familiar or strange jumped out at him.

Fergus muttered under his breath, telling himself to calm down and think rationally, but that frustration that rode his gut rose again. He had a debt to Samuel to learn the identity of his murderer, and his lack of progress ate at him. Nothing he'd done so far had helped piece together what had happened.

He entered the pub but halted inside the doorway, the weight of a stare enticing him to glance over his shoulder. The old man in the coat was frowning at him, but before Fergus could offer help, the man scuttled away and vanished around a corner. Strange. Fergus took a step back, then shrugged. The man wasn't important. It was time to ask Claire if she'd go out with him. He was ready to move on and forget the past, forget Miranda.

The pub bustled with loud chatter, laughter, and background music. Glasses and bottles clinked. Customers filled every available chair. Men clustered around a bar table, their beers within easy reach. The scent of fries and ketchup drifted to him, along with the meaty, tomato goodness of what he thought might be lasagna. He pushed through the crowd, deciding to position himself at the bar.

Claire pulled pints while another of her part-timers served wine to three dithering twenty-something-year-olds. Their high-pitched giggles plucked at Fergus's nerves, and he sidled along to the section where Claire worked, wedging between the local fire chief and a woman with an American accent.

Claire's smile lit her face when she saw him. She finished serving her customer and checked for anyone waiting before she moved nearer to him, limping a little. "I didn't think I'd see you tonight. I assumed you needed to catch up on work."

"After I checked in at the office, I had dinner with my family," Fergus said, wondering if it was indelicate to mention chafed thighs. At least, he assumed that was the problem. That and sore muscles from holding tight during the flight.

"How long has it been since you've seen them?"

"Almost a year." His brow furrowed as he thought back. "Actually, longer than that. I trained in Wellington and accepted a job in Dunedin because it was the only option."

"Your family lives in Auckland, right?"

"Yes, they had plenty of police officers in the Auckland region, so I went south. From Dunedin, I worked in Invercargill before I ended up here."

"In all the time you've spent coming in here, you've never voluntarily mentioned anything personal. Why now?" A hint of wonder threaded through her voice.

"My secrets are fewer now," he said with an edge of dryness.

Claire laughed, and he grinned back, his heart unexpectedly light.

"Do you want to join me on Thursday? If the weather holds, we could pack a picnic and fly into the mountains."

Claire beamed. "Yes! Thank you. I'd love that. I never get time to do the longer walks. Today was the first time I'd set foot anywhere near Mount Luxmore and the Luxmore hut. The view up there is incredible." She paused and pulled a face, glancing left and right before she leaned closer to whisper, "My legs are killing me."

"A hot bath should help that." Lightness filled Fergus's chest. "I'll call you with a time closer to the day. If the weather changes, we can watch a movie or eat out."

Claire nodded. "Sounds fantastic. Oops, a customer."

"I need to go, anyway. I want to walk a circuit of the town." With a grin that he was positive lurked near dopey, Fergus waved and strode for the door. The thrill of the coming excursion with Claire flared within him. Rightness. His phone vibrated, and he glanced at the screen.

Miranda.

Again.

He stared at the unoriginal message. She wanted him back and was sorry for her behavior.

Fergus dragged in an audible breath and tapped in a reply. *Miranda, I'm seeing someone else. You married and moved on, and so have I. It's time for you to forget about us and stop contacting me.*

He reread his message and hit send before continuing home. He hesitated briefly at the road's end before turning right toward the town center. Perhaps he'd pick up the strange, frustrating scent. The trail's elusiveness was peculiar.

Nothing unusual, although he scared a group of young men intending to drive while intoxicated. One peek at him, and they called for a ride. He lingered until they left with an older sibling before heading home.

Physically exhausted but in a fantastic mood, Fergus unlocked his door and entered his home. With his keen dragon sight, he didn't need to switch on a light. He undressed and slid into bed, his mind still busy with the puzzle and frustrated at his lack of clues.

No one had seen anything, heard anything. The crime scene had provided no clues except the weird scent, the foreign hair, and the swarm of flies. Samuel's body had yielded little either, apart from the knowledge his assailant had stabbed him. Fergus pondered the matter and planned what to check the next day. Finding out what happened to Samuel was his top priority.

A funeral.

The thought blasted through him without warning.

Dragons never buried their dead. They burned them, and he thought werewolves did something similar. He'd check with Iain tomorrow and ensure he sent Samuel's spirit on the last journey with dignity.

Fergus called Iain early the following day to discuss Samuel.

"We should wrap him in a shroud and fly him high into the mountains. An old werewolf would like to know he became one with nature. I can speak the old tongue, and you and Elspeth can fire him."

"I spoke to Nikau earlier, and he told me the body is ready for release. Can we do this for Samuel this morning?"

"Hang on. I'll check with Elspeth."

Fergus heard Iain's low rumble but didn't discern the words. He thought his mother spoke in the background.

"Where is the body? Should we meet you at the police station?"

"I'll collect Samuel now and take him to my place. I'll meet you there."

Half an hour later, they were on their way. Fergus led, carrying Samuel's body while Elspeth ferried Iain on her back. It was a fabulous, crisp day with little wind, and except for their purpose, Fergus would've enjoyed flying with his sister and brother-in-law. He had a particular cave in mind, where he had sought refuge for two days during a sudden weather change. The isolated area meant nobody would notice or be concerned about the smoke. The site would remain undisturbed, leaving Samuel's spirit free to wander the mountaintops. At least, that was what Fergus liked to think.

They flew over the Kepler Track, and several trampers gazed at them. Fergus continued flying for half an hour before changing trajectory and arrowing downward toward a mountain slope. He landed, and Elspeth settled beside him.

Iain clambered down, and he and Elspeth shifted to their human forms, each undeterred by the chill in the air.

"This spot is perfect," Iain declared, scanning the cave's mouth, the mountain peaks, and the alpine lake beyond. Trees covered the lower slopes before they gave way to rocks and drifts of snow.

"No one will disturb him here." Fergus carefully picked

up the shroud and carried it to the cave mouth. He set his old friend down, bowing his head briefly in a silent show of respect.

Elspeth and Iain stepped up beside Fergus, their mood somber.

Fergus broke the silence first. "Samuel, my old friend, I wish I knew what happened. Rest assured I'll discover the identity of the person who murdered you. I will not stop until I discern the truth. You were a good man, a staunch friend, and I will miss you. My garden has never looked so fine, and I valued our time together."

Iain chanted in a language Fergus didn't recognize, but he sensed the power and sincerity. The intent. The words echoed inside the cave and resounded back, creating an eerie double effect. As the mantra trailed into silence, Iain shifted, flowing into his wolf form. He lifted his shaggy reddish-brown head and howled.

Fergus's skin erupted in goosebumps. This was spiritual and right. The perfect send-off for Samuel.

Iain ended his howl, and the three of them stood in respectful silence for a minute longer.

"Fergus, are you ready?" Elspeth asked.

"Yes."

Iain stepped back while his wife and Fergus shifted to dragon. "Farewell, my friend," Fergus said silently, dragging in a draft of breath. An instant later, it whooshed back out along with a flare of dragon fire. Elspeth mirrored his actions. The shroud caught fire, and in seconds, it was ablaze. Fergus and Elspeth continued forcing their fire at Samuel's body until it burned bright and disintegrated to ash.

Sadness weighed down Fergus as he backed out of the cave and exited the shadows.

Outside, Iain stood unnaturally still, his head cocked while he listened intently. Fergus frowned, hearing nothing out of the ordinary. His gaze slid to Elspeth. She remained motionless, also listening.

Fergus gave up trying to hear whatever sound was perplexing Iain and shifted. He pulled out the thermos his mother had given to Elspeth. Another container held cups, and a third produced half a dozen homemade chocolate chip cookies. While he arranged the cups and poured the fragrant hot chocolate, he watched Iain and Elspeth.

Each remained in their animal form, but he could tell by the tilt of his sister's head they were communicating telepathically. His mother and father also communicated this way, and Fergus grinned, remembering a day when he and Elspeth were children. They'd all been fiercely independent and often ran in different directions at the same time. Their mother had lamented that she had to restrain her yells to one more suitable for a human instead of letting fly with a dragon roar.

In the dragon world, only soul mates could communicate mind-to-mind.

He and Miranda had never managed this feat. The thought no longer carried the same sting, and the pain of Miranda's betrayal had dulled.

Since Claire.

Iain and Elspeth were still absorbed. "What's up?" he

asked. "Your hot chocolate is getting cold."

Elspeth shifted. "Iain is positive he heard a wolf call in reply to his tribute to Samuel. We've been listening, but it hasn't repeated."

"Drink your hot chocolate, and we'll try calling out once we've finished," Fergus suggested. "You know Ma will ask how we enjoyed the cookies."

"Or there will be a note underneath that we won't see because she's sneaky that way," Elspeth added, grabbing clothes and hastily donning them.

Iain shifted and shook his head. "You do that to our boys with their school lunches. Now I know where you learned it."

"Did you get a location for the wolf call?" Fergus asked. "Apart from you, Finn, and Samuel, no other wolves exist in the area."

"Pinpointing the direction was challenging due to the swirling wind and mountains distorting and echoing. The call sounded..." His gaze went distant.

"What?" Fergus prompted.

"The howl sounded like a distress signal."

10

It was late afternoon when Fergus and Elspeth flew back into town. Fergus returned to the police station while Iain and Elspeth headed home to reclaim their children.

The first thing Fergus did was review his messages in case anything required immediate attention.

Old Mrs. McGregor's querulous voice filled his office. "Those boys are raiding my apple orchard again. If you don't arrest them, I'll take matters into my own hands."

Fergus winced at the thump of her old phone. Given the abrupt crunch, he'd bet the handpiece had jumped back out of the cradle. The next message began.

"Paul William here. I've just driven home and almost hit a cow. Six wandering cattle, near the old Jones place by the lake."

Fergus scowled at this news. Loose cattle were dangerous to kids walking home from school and motorists. He listened to the rest of the calls and decided he could deal with them tomorrow, but if the cattle were still roaming, he needed to speak with their owner and read them the riot act. A hapless walker might've left a gate open since that had happened before. He'd reserve judgment until he scoped out the situation. Mrs. McGregor lived in the same direction, which meant he could stop in on her and reassure her he'd speak to the likely culprits.

His phone rang as he drove toward the lakeside farm to check on the stray cattle. He answered using Bluetooth. "Officer Murray."

"Fergus," Elspeth snapped. "We need you at the children's playground right now."

"What's happened?" he demanded, alerted by the angry mother-bear tone.

"A man tried to abduct Niall and Connor."

"The playground on the lake?"

"Yes," she said tersely, fear leaking through her reply.

"Stay there and keep calm. I'll be there in a few minutes." He shut off his sister's indignant squawk and did a U-turn. Seconds later, he was on his way to the lakefront playground, which was popular with local kids and visitors. He spotted his family straight away. Although they were trying not to be obvious, they had Niall and Connor in a protective circle.

Fergus strode over to them. They all spoke at once, and he held up his right hand in a stop motion. He enforced this with his words. "I'll speak to the boys first, then the rest of you. Okay?" He focused on Elspeth, who was fairly vibrating with motherly rage, although one glance told him the two kids seemed unharmed. "Elspeth?"

"Yes." The word was an explosion of fury, but she stood aside to let Fergus crouch beside his nephews.

"Did you have fun this afternoon?" he asked and swished his hand to stop a fly from settling on his cheek. His eyes widened. Purple. Before he could react, the insect buzzed away, and he lost sight of it. He hadn't seen any of these flies since the day he'd discovered Samuel. Frowning, he focused on the boys while hoping like hell he wasn't gonna find another body in the vicinity.

Niall, the oldest boy and a carbon copy of Iain with his curly brown hair and blue eyes, nodded at his question. Once he matured, the boy would be as tall as his father.

"Yes," he said. "Connor and I ran with four legs and played soccer with the big dogs. It was lots of fun."

Fergus grinned even as he hoped the dogs' owners appreciated his nephews' easy-going nature. They'd inherited their laid-back attitude from Iain as well. Elspeth had always had a bit of a temper. "Then what did you do?"

His youngest nephew, Connor, piped up. He took after Elspeth with his light brown straight hair and brown eyes. "We shifted, and Grandma made us put on our clothes before we could play with the humans."

"It's important to fit in with the humans and not scare them," Fergus agreed.

Niall frowned. "But everyone has a naked body beneath their clothes. Grandma didn't explain why we need clothes."

Fergus bit back the humor that flashed through him. He'd preferred to run around naked as a child. "Nakedness

136

makes some humans uncomfortable. If we want to fit in, it's best to follow the rules."

A furrow appeared between Connor's brown eyes. "Even if they're wrong?"

"Yes," Elspeth snapped from behind Fergus.

Fergus shot her a warning look. "You put on clothes and played with the other children?"

"Yes," Niall agreed. "We played until our tummies got hungry. The other kids left with their parents."

"But you and Connor kept playing alone on the slide and the swings?"

His nephews nodded, their eyes huge.

"What happened next?"

"Grandma and Grandpa had gone for a walk. We waited by the table where they'd left the pack with our food and our ball. We could see them, and they waved at us," Niall said.

"Did you see anyone else nearby?" Fergus asked.

"A man was sitting at the next table," Connor said.

"Two other children came with their mother and were playing on the swings," Niall replied. "They didn't stay for long because their father came. They were going for ice cream." This last emerged with a trace of wistfulness.

"What did the man do?"

"The man came closer and started talking to us."

"I see," Fergus said. His parents had probably been watching the kids from a distance, but the man's appearance hadn't upset them unduly. "What did he say?"

"He asked if we were hungry," Niall said.

"We said we were," Connor added. "I'm still hungry."

The kid's stomach rumbled on cue to back up his words.

Elspeth muttered something from behind Fergus, but his mother produced two large cookies and handed one to each child.

"What did the man say when you told him you were hungry?" Fergus's gut clenched, and he could guess what might come next, but he had to ask anyway.

"He said there was an ice cream shop down the road, and he'd buy us one. We could come right back with our ice creams. That's what he said," Connor said.

"But Mummy told us never to accept food or gifts from a stranger," Niall said. "I didn't want to go, but my stomach did. It kept growling."

"What about your wolf?" Fergus asked. "What did your wolf tell you?"

"He said the man smelled funny. Like danger and blood," Connor said slowly.

Iain, who stood beside them, exchanged a glance with Fergus. He took over the questioning, and Fergus let him because his brother-in-law would know which questions to ask to rattle free the answers they sought. It couldn't be a coincidence, surely?

"Can you tell me again what the man smelled like?" Iain asked his two sons. "So I can recognize him if I see him."

Niall frowned, his brow puckering. "Funny."

At his side, Connor reminded Fergus strongly of Elspeth. The same determined concentration. The peek of his tongue at the corner of his mouth.

"Was it a good funny or a bad funny scent?" Iain asked, his gaze on Connor.

"It's hard to describe," Connor said after glancing at his brother. "We smelled old blood like the man hadn't washed behind his ears or cleaned his nails after a kill." He looked at his mother. "Will he grow potatoes in his ears?"

"Quite possibly," Elspeth said. "After I have a word with him."

"Elspeth," Fergus said, his tone sharp and signaling her to shut up.

She opened her mouth to argue.

"Elspeth, please," Iain said in an equally abrupt tone. "This is important."

Elspeth snapped her teeth together, but her silence would come with a cost. Fergus knew it, and no doubt Iain understood this too.

"Connor, is there anything else about the man's scent that was different?" Iain asked.

"Why?"

Fergus pressed his lips together, amused. In the short time his nephews had been in Te Anau, he'd learned of their need to understand everything, ranging from how things worked to why they needed to carry out parental instructions.

"Because we think this is a dangerous man who killed an old werewolf. We would like to speak to the man who offered you ice cream," Fergus said.

Either his mother or father or perhaps his sister made a soft sound of protest, but neither Iain nor Fergus turned to check on the source of the objection.

"He smelled like a predator," Connor said finally.

"His smell was new," Niall said.

139

That puzzled Fergus until Iain said, "You haven't come across a scent like that before."

The boys nodded.

"His eyes glowed funny," Niall added. "The man scared my wolf."

"All right," Fergus said. "Can you tell me what he looked like?"

"He was old," Niall said.

"Older than Mum and Dad?" Fergus asked.

"Yes," Connor confirmed. "He had black hair. He tucked it under his jacket, but it looked long."

"Smart clothes," Niall added, his eyes brighter now.

"Smart, how?" Iain asked.

Connor gestured in front of his body. "Going out clothes. Important ones."

"Like a suit?" Fergus prompted.

"Yes, black jacket. Black trousers. White shirt. Like Daddy wears when he goes to a special place for dinner."

"You'd think a guy in a suit would grab attention," Iain murmured. "Most people down here are pretty casual—tourists from overseas, visitors from New Zealand. You'd think he'd stand out."

"What about his face?" Fergus asked, hoping for more from his nephews but understanding this was a long shot.

Connor and Niall exchanged glances, and Niall spoke for his younger brother. "He had old skin. Wrinkles. And a funny thing with hairs on his chin. Like a freckle." Niall tapped the left side of his jaw.

"A mole?" Iain asked.

Connor shrugged. "It had black hairs growing from it."

"How tall was he? As tall as me?"

Connor studied Fergus and shook his head. "He was the same as Mummy, but sometimes he leaned forward."

Fergus had no idea what that meant, but he had enough to canvas the area and check with parents with children playing here. Someone had to have seen something. "Good job, Connor. Niall. How about I take you for a walk now, and I'll buy you an ice cream?"

Connor jumped and clapped his hands while Niall gave a human version of a howl.

"You'll spoil their dinner," Elspeth complained.

"No," Dougal said, stepping in to still his daughter's protest. "The boys did well in this situation, and we should reward them for not going off with a stranger. Who knows what might've happened if the kids had ignored their instincts and accepted an ice cream from this man."

Elspeth clenched and unclenched her hands, her tight expression telling Fergus her imagination was in overdrive. "You're right, of course. Thanks, Fergus. We're going back to the house. Can you bring the boys home as soon as you're done? They need to have a bath before dinner."

"I'll go with them," Iain said. "I wouldn't mind an ice cream myself."

Fergus and Iain ushered the boys in front of them. They ran ahead, but not too far to worry Fergus.

"Do you think other kids are in danger?" Iain asked in an undertone.

"I don't know. Te Anau is usually a quiet town with no trouble. I deal with a few drunks and the occasional fight. The odd search and rescue op when hikers get lost or injured. This month, I've had a murder, and now this. Maybe it's something in the water."

"It can't happen again. We were lucky this time," Iain said.

"Yes." Fergus's tone was grim. "Damn, this is frustrating. We're running blind here. All we can do is watch and wait."

"We should do another circuit of the town tonight," Iain said.

"Did you check for a scent around the swings and at the picnic tables?"

Iain cursed softly. "I followed the scent briefly, but from what Dougal and Fiona said, the park was busy earlier. I couldn't find the man's trail."

"Tomorrow, I'll reconnoiter the hotels and other accommodation. Maybe I'll get lucky, and someone can identify this mystery man. He must be a visitor to the area because I would've recognized him from the boys' description. I'll check in with the local school principal and inform him of what happened. He can get the word out and warn parents and kids about stranger danger."

"What can I do to help?" Iain asked. "I need a task to keep busy instead of worrying about my sons."

"We have dozens of hotels and motels in Te Anau. It will take time to speak to the owners of every business. I'll give you a signed letter of approval to seek information on my behalf, and we'll take half each. If you find this guy—no throttling or beating. We must do this legally."

Iain released a gusty sigh. "Spoilsport."

Fergus grinned, but he didn't like this recent

development. Te Anau had never been a dangerous town, yet it felt like one now. "Can I drop you at the house? I have roaming cattle to deal with before they cause an accident."

"Yeah, thanks. I want to spend time with my boys and reassure myself they're safe."

Fergus got that. He did. What in the hell was happening to his tranquil town?

11

"FERGUS," HIS MOTHER SAID when he answered his phone. "Come for dinner. Iain is firing up the barbecue."

"Another time," Fergus said, scanning the official notices regarding crime in Manapouri, Queenstown, and the smaller towns farther afield. Few of them had a resident cop, but it had occurred to him he should study crimes outside of his town. He should've considered it before because criminals didn't confine themselves to one area. No murders, but theft seemed rampant.

"Fergus, are you listening?"

"No, I can't come to dinner. I have other plans."

"What?"

"Ma, I'm an adult." Fergus stopped speaking, wise to his mother's tricks by now.

"Are you going out with Claire?"

Fergus hesitated, and then it was too late. His mother pounced.

"You are!" she gushed. "I'm so pleased."

"Ma! I'm trying to work. See you tomorrow." Fergus hung up before his mother could sneak in another question.

He checked his watch because he'd arranged to pick up Claire. Given the strange occurrences of the last week, he didn't want her walking around town on her own.

Claire was ready when he pulled up in her driveway. She wore a dress that bared her arms in deference to the heat.

"You look pretty," he said, opening the car door for her.

"Thanks." A delicate flush bloomed in her cheeks, but she met his gaze without hesitation.

Fergus immediately wanted to kiss her. He hesitated, then thought, what the hell. He closed the distance between them and placed his hands on her shoulders, drawing her nearer and inhaling a flowery perfume. Their gazes connected and held, then his lips were on hers. She tasted sweet and willing, like she belonged to him.

Chauvinistic, much? Probably. *Definitely.*

He admitted the truth to himself.

He wanted her.

Once was *not* enough.

Aware of their situation—standing in her driveway in public view—and the passing time, he stepped back to allow her to get into the vehicle. Once she settled, he closed the door and trotted to the driver's side.

"What are we having for dinner?" she asked, her voice bright.

"I thought I'd barbecue steaks at home. Less chance of interruptions."

"Sounds good."

"Did you have trouble getting someone to cover for you? I figure Valerie hasn't appeared yet because you would've told me."

"No." Her dark brows drew together, and she grimaced. "No sign of Finn or James?"

"It's not like them to go off and not contact my parents or Iain and Elspeth. I flew over the mountains early this morning, hoping to see them."

"Nothing?" she asked.

"No." Fergus drove at the speed limit, his gaze sweeping the sidewalk for anything suspicious. This used to drive Miranda crazy, especially when they went for dinner. She'd hated him working as a cop.

"Am I allowed to ask about your murder inquiry?" she asked. "I will keep anything you tell me confidential."

Fergus trusted her, which gave him pause. He'd never discussed his work with Miranda, yet he instinctively understood Claire would never repeat anything. "Nothing much happening on that front. I feel as if I'm treading water. A tramper left a gate open at the farm on the southern side of the lake. Six steers got loose and caused chaos with the traffic. We've had a few burglaries, which is unusual."

He pulled up in front of his house.

"We don't have a problem with theft."

"That's what makes it so strange. The neighboring towns have had a larger number of burglaries, too."

He climbed out of his police car and trotted around the hood to open the door for her.

146

"Thank you," she said, her smile slow and intimate and doing things to his insides. That urge to kiss her nibbled at him again, but he was also hungry. Maybe after dinner.

Fergus locked his vehicle and guided her up the front path. The pots of petunias appeared ragged and droopy because he'd forgotten to water them. Sam had always taken care of that.

He pushed away the spurt of grief that pierced his heart and urged Claire inside.

"Wow," she said, noting the table already set for two. "You're organized."

"I never know when a call will come in, and it has made me think ahead and use every minute when I want to achieve something."

She cocked her head, interest in her blue eyes. She'd left her hair loose tonight, and his fingers itched to test the silkiness and learn if his memories were accurate.

"Do you have regular callouts?"

"It's hard to predict. Can I get you something to drink? A glass of wine or a juice?"

"White wine?"

"I have sauvignon blanc," he said.

"Yes, please. Can I do anything to help?"

"All organized," he said, and that would be true as soon as he turned on the oven to finish baking the potatoes.

"These burglaries. Are they confined to an area? What sort of things are the thieves taking? Is it bored teens?"

"Mainly food and drinks, but also clothes. Marion Baker and her husband arrived home from their Australian holiday to find someone had stripped their pantry of canned goods. They'd emptied their wardrobes, too. Mrs. McGregor's orchard keeps getting raided. She's positive it's the teenagers who walk past after the school bus drop, but I'm not convinced."

"Wow," Claire said.

"Yep," Fergus said, crossing to the fridge to pull out a bottle of wine. He filled two glasses and handed one to Claire. "Come and sit in the lounge." Usually, he'd suggest sitting on the rear verandah overlooking the garden, but Samuel's murder was still so raw. He couldn't bear to recall the metallic scent of blood and kept seeing Samuel's body in his mind's eye, lying in the vegetable patch.

Claire followed him into the lounge and sank onto the two-seater. She sipped her wine before fixing him with a gimlet eye.

Fergus stiffened, every dragon instinct flaring to life.

"Why did you friend-zone me? And then ask me out tonight?"

Oh, boy. Fergus hesitated. What to tell her? Did he say he wasn't sure if he could commit to anything more than casual lovers?

"Fergus, it's a simple question."

And now he'd irked her.

Well, hell. He tasted his wine to stall.

"Don't tell me then." She rose, but he grabbed her arm as she flounced past.

"Please don't leave."

She shook herself free and sat, waiting in dignified silence.

Okay, the truth it was, then.

"I was engaged to be married before I arrived in Te Anau. Miranda hated the small-town life and only came for the odd weekend when I worked in Invercargill."

"Invercargill is a city," Claire said, indignant.

"Miranda preferred big city life and wanted someone with more money. She met a man—a billionaire—in Auckland. He could give her what I couldn't, and after she broke off our engagement, she went to him. She married him not long afterward."

Claire said nothing, and Fergus fell silent, tossed back in those dark times. He'd loved Miranda so much, but in hindsight, she'd been using him. He wasn't even sure why she'd accepted his proposal because he didn't think she'd ever truly wanted him, not even before she knew he was a dragon. And he was fudging the truth…

"Bitch," Claire said, breaking the silence.

Fergus barked out a laugh.

"Well, she is," Claire said. "You're a good man."

"Ah, but I'm not a man. When I told Miranda I was a dragon, she didn't deal well with that disclosure. We stayed together for a few more months, but our relationship wasn't working. I scared Miranda. My dragon status was the main reason we broke up."

"Why?"

"She thought I'd injure her."

Claire snorted. "That's ridiculous. Did she know you at all?"

Warmth suffused his chest, a living, breathing thing. Claire trusted him, and she was friendly with his parents and family. Iain and Elspeth approved of her. His gaze shot to her pink lips. He stood and crossed the floor to sit on the two-seater beside her.

Fergus removed the wineglass clutched in her hand and set it aside. Then he hauled her onto his knee and kissed her, pouring every ounce of thankfulness and relief into the exchange. At first, her body remained stiff, and he second-guessed himself. Had he frightened her?

Gradually, she relaxed, kissing him back and pressing nearer. When Fergus pulled away, they were both breathing hard.

"How hungry are you?" he asked, eyeing her closely.

Her grin came slowly, and it was damn sexy, that knowing expression doing things to him. "Why?"

"I want to strip those clothes off your sexy body and make love to you. No other reason."

"Oh."

"Is that yes or no?"

She never hesitated. "Yes."

Fergus rose, taking her weight as he stood. Long strides took him down a passage to his bedroom, where he placed her on her feet.

"Let me undress you."

"Please."

"I thought you might argue," he said, not hiding his surprise. He hadn't genuinely thought that she'd give him full trust like this. Miranda hadn't. He stared at her, part of him waiting for her to reconsider, to recall that she was a human and he was not.

Her brow crinkled, and he saw the second that understanding reached her. A flash of temper sped across her face. Indignation. "I'm not her," she snapped. Her chest rose and fell as she inhaled and exhaled. The breathing seemed to calm her, and her expression softened. "She hurt you. Trampled on your heart. I get it, but you've known me for months. I like to think that I treat everyone the same and fairly. It doesn't make any difference that you're a dragon. You serve the people of this town. Your paranormal status doesn't change this, right?"

Fergus's throat closed with emotion and gratitude. He'd liked Claire since they'd first met, and his dragon had given him grief for creeping out of the Queenstown hotel room. Meeting her again...sometimes it had been difficult leaving her in the friend zone.

"Fergus?"

He ran his hands up her arms and cradled her face. She didn't flinch or react with disgust. Instead, she met his gaze, her blue one radiating defiance and determination. He pressed his forehead to hers, breathing in her scent.

"Thank you," he whispered. "Thank you for trusting me with your safety."

"Fergus." This time her voice was chiding.

She stepped away from him, pulling from his touch. For a fleeting second, he thought this was a rejection, but humor morphed on her face. A hint of sassy flirtation as she whipped her pink T-shirt over her head to reveal the lacy pink bra beneath. His breath caught, his hands falling to his sides, and he couldn't have ceased watching if he'd tried.

Claire did a little shimmy and wriggled her denim skirt over her hips.

Fergus licked his lips, wanting to purr along with his dragon because she wore matching pink panties.

She glanced at him and fluttered her eyelashes. "Can you take it from here, or would you like me to continue?"

Fergus lunged, scooping her off her feet and tossing her on the bed. He was on her in a blink, and to his relief, she didn't show a trace of fear. He stilled to give her yet another chance to protest, then rapidly removed his blue uniform shirt.

"All off," Claire said firmly.

Fergus grinned. He loved a confident and assertive woman. To keep the lady happy, he removed his socks, trousers, and underwear, tossing the garments on a handy chair.

"Nice," she said. "I didn't have a chance to gawk last time."

Fergus snorted before getting serious. "I don't want to lose our friendship."

"Who says we will? Let's enjoy the now instead of worrying about the future."

"You're right," Fergus said. Besides, being with Claire like this felt right.

With Miranda, he'd always felt like she was judging him. He'd had to accede to her wishes; otherwise, she sulked, and the woman held a mean grudge. His family hadn't taken to Miranda, although they'd always been welcoming and polite. They liked Claire.

Fergus shoved off his remaining doubts because he and his dragon were on the same page. They wanted Claire. He kissed her, holding back none of the yearning, the tenderness, the need that dwelled within him. She let him be himself, and that was freeing.

He almost cheered when he felt one arm wind around his neck and the other clutch his shoulder, holding him close. In the next instant, she was pushing him away.

He stilled. "Something wrong?"

"Nope," she chirped. "But I have a sudden urge to be on top."

Fergus wordlessly complied, shifting his body to free her before lying flat on the mattress. She straddled his hips, a devilish smile on her lips as she started to explore. She ran her hands over his chest and dipped her head to kiss and lick and nibble.

He started at the scoring of her teeth over his pectoral muscle, his pulse jumping and his blood pooling at his groin. Unable to resist, he ran his hands through her hair, which *was* as silky as he remembered. She sat back and reached behind to unfasten her bra, drawing his attention. She grinned as she tossed it aside to reveal her creamy breasts.

"I love your curves. You are stunning," he whispered.

The faint blush in her cheeks told him his compliment had thrown her, but he meant every word. He didn't subscribe to empty flattery.

"And I like confident men with muscles and sexy smiles," she said, slyly rubbing her butt against his erection. "How do you feel about fast and furious?" Her stomach rumbled. "I'm a little hungry."

Fergus went to slide off the bed, but she stopped him with a small hand in the middle of his chest.

"No. I want sex more. Right now."

He fell back and stared up at her. "Your panties are in the way."

"One of us will need to move to get a condom," she said with a shrug. "That can be me."

"Multi-tasking is good."

"Exactly," she said. "Condoms?"

"There's a packet in the bedside cabinet." He jerked his head to indicate which one.

Claire jumped up and yanked open the drawer. She pulled out the new packet of Fancy Free condoms he'd purchased with his groceries during a quick trip to Queenstown a few days ago. The last thing he'd wanted was to cause gossip amongst the Te Anau population. More gossip, although it occurred to him that if he and Claire openly dated, it might calm the more suspicious locals. They might see him as less of a threat if they were a couple.

"It's a new packet," she said.

"Claire, I haven't been with anyone since Queenstown."

She blinked. "Really?"

"Yes." And now he wondered if his subconscious was working in tandem with his dragon.

"I haven't either." She handed him the condoms and stepped out of her panties.

Fergus did an up-and-down scan and hurriedly opened the box. He pulled out a strip.

Claire held out her hand. "I'll do the honors."

Thankfully, she didn't dawdle or tease him but rolled the rubber down his shaft. She straddled him again and leaned down to kiss him. This one was sweet and sexy and had him groaning and reaching for her. She shifted a fraction, rising on her knees, and he watched avidly as she took him inside her. Slowly and torturously.

"I thought you wanted fast?" he said.

Once fully seated, she opened her eyes to stare at him or judge his reaction, and then she winked.

"Oh, I intend on quick." Her whisper was full of erotic promise as she lifted her body, his cock dragging along her inner walls.

He shivered and shut up, content to watch the seductive picture she made. So sexy. His. *Theirs.*

She increased her pace, rising and falling faster now, one of her hands delving between her thighs to give herself increased stimulation.

Fergus gazed at her, entranced with the bounce of her breasts, the subtle sexiness of her curvy body, and her confidence. The sexual tension in him ramped up, especially when she paused briefly to caress his balls, the gentle scoring almost undoing him when she clamped down on his cock.

He hissed, his need surging.

"Move. Please," he said.

"My pleasure."

Claire bore down, her movements rapid and her breathing coming faster. He delighted in the play of emotions over her face, even as he struggled to let her remain in control.

"Yes," Claire said with a groan.

And he felt the rapid grip and release of his shaft, the

added stimulation too much for him. He gripped her hips for purchase and surged up, his strokes rapid and a fine sheen of sweat coating his body. His hips rose, and he came with a convulsive heave of muscles. He held himself still, and along with the surge of pleasure, he experienced the tiny spasms of her body.

She was magnificent.

She fell forward, and he wrapped his arms around her, utterly content.

This was going to happen again. He'd make sure of it. Somehow, Claire had snuck into the empty spaces in his heart. This needed some serious thinking...

12

FERGUS SAT WITH IAIN at a café with a coffee and muffin, frustration a heavy ball in the pit of his stomach. He and Iain had spoken to the hotel manager on the lakefront, where Iain had first encountered the gamey smell, but she hadn't recognized the guest from their description.

"I'm no further ahead with learning who murdered Samuel or locating Playground Man." He wasn't sure what to do next.

"How did the date with Claire go?" Iain asked. "Your mother and Elspeth told me to ask."

Fergus rolled his eyes and ignored the spurt of warmth in his chest. "They thought getting you to pry would work? You can tell them my private life is none of their business. No, wait. Don't tell them anything. They can ask me if they want information."

Iain grinned, his blue eyes sparkling with humor at Fergus's expense. "You'll tell them what?"

"Nothing," Fergus confirmed. "My life is confidential."

"They'll set their sights on Claire next," Iain warned.

Fergus pulled a face. "When are you returning to Auckland?"

"Not sure." Something in his tone had Fergus scrutinizing him more closely.

"You might not return?"

Iain shrugged. "Elspeth and I have been talking. We love it here. The wide, open spaces appeal to us, and the boys love running around in both forms. The locals have been a little standoffish, but they'll return greetings, which is a start. Property is much cheaper here than in Auckland."

Fergus nodded his understanding. Even though his family's arrival had outed him, the locals continued bringing their problems to him. Yes, some idiot had tagged the police station with witty warnings such as *Dragon, go home*. Fergus ignored them since most citizens had acted with wariness but had soon relaxed when he'd behaved no differently. Despite his frustration with his family, this new openness might be beneficial. Now, he could use his dragon talents in search and rescue operations instead of sneaking around.

"What about Mum and Dad? Finn and James? Are they intending to go back to Auckland?

"Dougal and Fiona don't have the same problems where they live since many of the residents are of paranormal origin," Iain said. "But we haven't discussed our return yet. We'd planned to drive down to Invercargill and cross to Stewart Island. We thought we'd spend a week on the island." He frowned. "Finn and James aren't back yet."

Fergus shot him a sharp look. "Are Mum and Dad worried?"

"They're anxious but trying to hide it, I think. The boys knew we intended to head to Stewart Island and were keen to go with the rest of us."

"Not even meeting the girl would change that?"

"I don't think so because they knew we only intended to be away for a week."

A thought occurred to Fergus. "Iain," he said. "What if I'm looking at Samuel's murder wrong? What if paranormal species were the common factor in everything happening around here? Someone murdered Samuel—a werewolf. Connor and Niall are werewolves, and a stranger attempts to lure them away with ice cream. Now Finn and James are overdue returning from a trip into the mountains. What if someone is targeting those who have *other* blood?"

"We should speak with your parents. Elspeth. And we should keep an extra close eye on each other. You said no other paranormal beings live in the area, right?"

"Yeah. Now that Samuel has gone, I'm it. Watching each other is sensible," Fergus said.

Iain and Fergus finished their coffee and left. Their drive to the lakeside rental was tense, each man pondering the feasibility of Fergus's theory.

The two boys were playing outside, and Elspeth and his parents were watching them while stopping for a cup of tea.

"Fergus. Iain." His mother's smile faded. "What's wrong?"

Fergus dropped onto an empty seat, and Iain took a position against the supporting verandah beam near Elspeth.

"The morning you arrived, somebody murdered my werewolf friend Samuel. He died from stab wounds. A few days ago, a stranger tried to take Connor and Niall. Finn and James are overdue. I know they're adults and responsible, but it's not like them to take off. It occurred to me that these events might be connected because each involved has paranormal blood."

His father tapped his fingers on the tabletop, his brows drawn together in concentration. He ceased tapping, his gaze fixing on Fergus. "You think someone is killing paranormal beings?"

"Don't know. I'm not even sure if my theory is right. But I find the incidents odd. Unusual for my town. The scent that Iain picked up at the murder scene—I get brief flashes, the odd whiff, but it's not enough to track. My sense of smell is decent. Better than a human's. One other odd thing—we discovered hundreds of purple flies at the crime scene. When Nikau, our vet, took a closer look at them, he discovered they were mechanical. I saw a fly at the playground."

"I didn't notice flies," Elspeth said.

"There was only one."

His father drummed his fingers again. "A paranormal creature?"

"It's possible. Iain couldn't identify the scent, but he and the boys noted it as unusual."

"What do you want us to do?" his mother asked.

"We need to search for Finn and James," Fergus said. "And we should all take care if we're alone. It'd be better if we were always in pairs. Watch the boys closely."

"I'll call Auntie Mabel and get her to come," Elspeth said. "She is capable of watching Connor and Niall and keeping them safe. That way, I can help search for the boys."

"Does anyone know exactly where they were going?" Fergus asked. "The townsfolk saw them fly into the mountains. We searched for them, but it was impossible to guess their destination. The hikers saw them from the Luxmore Hut, and we don't know where they went after that. And Iain thought he heard a distress howl when we took Samuel's body to the mountains."

"We'll search their room. It might offer an insight. They were looking at maps and keen to explore the mountain region." His mother jumped to her feet, but Fergus stayed her with a hand signal.

"Mum, let me search. It's better if one of us searches carefully. If we all do it, we might miss something."

His search produced maps, books, and receipts from places around town. Fergus collected the receipts to scrutinize later, intending to build a picture of his brother's activities. Other than that, he found nothing useful.

But another thought occurred. He should search Valerie's room. It was an excellent excuse to revisit Claire. He'd called her several times, but she was short-staffed and unable to get away for another outing. Fergus had spent more time with his family, and the rest of his nights, he and

Iain had searched for the elusive suit-wearing man.

"Time for me to go," Fergus said. "I'll be back later and intend to fly. I'll do a grid pattern over the lake and nearby mountains. Meantime, if any of you can think of where they might have gone, let me know."

"Son, we'll help you," Dougal said.

"All of us," Elspeth said. "Iain can come with me as an extra pair of eyes."

"What about the boys?"

"Don't worry," his mother said. "Mabel is on the way. She'll be here in less than an hour."

Fergus blinked, then nodded acceptance. Although he'd been happy before his family arrived, having them at his back eased some of the burden on him. "Thanks, I appreciate the help."

Fergus walked directly to Claire's pub and found her behind the bar. "Do you have time for a quick chat?" he asked.

Claire's broad smile of greeting fell away. "Something work-related?"

Fergus hated bringing this to Claire and involving her even further because these anomalies in his town made his spidey senses spike. "Valerie lived on the premises, right?"

"She did," Claire said. "Do you have news?"

"No, but my family and I are worried. It's not like Finn and James to ghost us. I want to search Valerie's room for clues to help us find the three."

Claire hesitated. "Normally, I'd cite privacy, but I'm concerned about Valerie. She told me she has no family, and since she has no one to stand for her, I'm rather conflicted." She nibbled her bottom lip.

Instantly, his mind zapped to their recent night together, and he silently cursed the customers—the locals—watching them with eagle eyes. He sighed inwardly. Later. He'd carve out time with Claire later.

"I wouldn't ask you to let me search her room if it wasn't important." He hesitated, his mind clicking through the facts. No. Trust needed to go both ways. "You remember Samuel's murder?"

Claire stared at him. "Yes."

"Samuel was a werewolf. A few days ago, a man tried to entice my young nephews with an offer of ice cream." His jaw tightened. "I haven't been able to locate this man."

Claire gasped, clapping her hand against her chest, her eyes wide with shock. "Are they all right? Were they hurt?"

"No, they're fine. Thankfully, they'd paid heed to my sister's stranger danger lectures. My point is that they are werewolves. Now Finn, James, and Valerie haven't returned to town."

"A dragon and another werewolf," Claire whispered.

God, he adored intelligent women. "My thoughts exactly."

"If you wait until my barman returns from his break, I'll take you to Valerie's room," Claire said.

"Son," a voice boomed from behind him. "I decided I'd come for a beer and to see if you needed help," Dougal said.

Inspiration bloomed in Fergus. "Dad, how would you feel about taking over the bar for Claire while we search Valerie's room?"

"I couldn't ask you to do that," Claire said quickly.

Dougal rubbed his chin. "Claire, you'd be doing me a favor. I'm not used to such an extended period of holiday. The truth is I prefer to keep busy. I'd happily help as often as you'd let me. I have experience. You don't need to worry about that."

Claire glanced at Fergus, and he nodded encouragement.

"If you're positive it's not an imposition."

Dougal slipped behind the bar and waved them away. "Take your time. I'll be fine. Tending a bar is like riding a bike."

Claire forced a smile and headed for a private door. "Valerie's room is through here."

Valerie's room was comfortable, with a tiny lounge area and a basic en suite. It was tidy, with everything in its place. The thing that struck Fergus immediately was the lack of personal touches.

"How long did Valerie say she intended to stay in Te Anau?"

"We didn't discuss exact dates, although she hoped to return to Auckland to start at university. Varsity courses begin in March."

"A few months, then. Do you think it's usual for a woman of Valerie's age to keep her room so impersonal?"

"No," Claire said slowly, her gaze traveling the space. "There are no tour brochures, ticket stubs, magazines, or books. I mean, she might have read on a tablet or phone. I don't know, but she enjoyed reading, or at least that's what she told me."

Fergus nudged a battered brown suitcase with his foot

and squatted to open the lid. It was full of neatly folded clothes. "She hasn't even unpacked properly. It's not as if they're winter clothes. These shirts look appropriate for the season."

Claire dropped on the bed as he searched through the case. "That is odd. I mean, if I were staying here for a few months, I'd unpack everything. Most people would."

Fergus rose and strode to a wooden dresser. He opened each drawer and rifled through the contents, doing a quick but thorough search. Most drawers were empty, which didn't bode well for his hopes of discovering something to help him in his search. The wardrobe offered little help, either. With each piece of furniture searched, Fergus's hopes plummeted.

He scanned the room, his gaze snagging on the bed. Unless there were loose floorboards, the bed was the only place left.

"I'll strip the covers off and make this easier," Claire said.

Fergus went to the opposite side of the bed to help. First, they took a pillow each before tossing them aside. They hit the treasure trove when they got to the bottom sheet. Right at the foot of the bed, lying between the mattress cover and the sheet, was a manila folder. Fergus let out a hiss. If he'd searched on his own, he would've probably lifted the mattress for signs of anything hidden under the bed and missed this. Fergus carefully removed the folder and flipped it open. It contained letters, copies of emails, and photos of people he didn't know. He noted a younger Valerie standing between an older couple. Her parents? He couldn't see any resemblance, but that didn't mean much.

Genetics sometimes played tricks.

He picked up the letter from the top of the pile and scanned the contents.

"Do you think we should read the documents? What if it's private?" Claire asked, hovering nearby.

"At this stage, Valerie and the boys are missing. No one knows their location, and they've been gone for too long. They're sensible kids, and this behavior is unusual."

Claire bit her lip, his confidence in the youngsters not reassuring her.

Fergus read the first page, then another, and cursed.

"What is it?" Claire pressed closer, attempting to read over his shoulder.

"Someone is blackmailing her," he said, his voice dark.

"I can't do it," Valerie said, her voice quivering with distress. "It's not right." Her hands moved at her sides in a restless motion, never settling. "I've done everything you told me to do. Everything, including luring those poor boys here, and now you want me to help you torture them? I can't do it, I tell you. I won't."

The woman—Karen Mercer—showed not a scrap of pity. Her big amber gaze hadn't moved from Valerie since she'd issued the order to inject Finn and James with the drug half an hour ago. Valerie glanced at the pair and shuddered; every part of her tense while a warning reverberated in her mind like a piercing alarm.

Whatever ingredients in the drug had turned them

into sexual beings, and they stared at her like ravening dogs. Valerie swallowed, her mouth trembling no matter how hard she bit her lower lip. She ran her clammy palms down her jeans, desperate to find a way out of this situation. Something. Anything. James kept blurring, shifting rapidly back and forth until his naked body trembled repeatedly. Finn wasn't as bad but wasn't his usual self, his normally bright eyes dull and his face pale.

"You will go in there and collect their sperm. I don't care how you do it, but you will carry out my orders, or I will kill your mother." The pitiless voice didn't change but emerged with robotic crispness and a complete lack of passion.

Valerie sagged, her body rounding inward. She was helpless. No matter which course of action she chose, someone would get hurt. She liked and admired Finn and James. They were fun-loving guys, but what she felt for them was friendship. Nothing more. She'd told them that upfront, and they'd accepted her decision to remain friends. That had made it easier to betray them because she'd kept her emotions tightly contained. At least, that had been the plan.

But now, this situation was a nightmare.

Valerie followed every one of Karen's instructions. She'd believed Karen when she'd told her she'd release her parents if Valerie did everything she said.

Karen had lied.

One lie after the other until Valerie became as trapped as her adopted parents. As trapped as Finn and James.

"I'll gut your mother first, and if you still resist, your

father is next."

The total lack of emotion and those flat amber eyes told Valerie the woman spoke the truth. She wouldn't hesitate—anything to further her crazy scheme.

A sob of frustration and anguish tore from Valerie, and the tightness in her chest made it difficult to breathe. She stared at Karen, her vision blurry from welling tears. "Why? Why are you doing this to me?"

Karen sniffed. "Because I can. Because it's necessary for my research. I'm almost at a breakthrough. I can feel it," she said and hissed.

Valerie flinched, surprised as Karen had never answered questions before. Eyes wide, she edged back because that hiss of Karen's was like a tic. A tell. It meant the woman was close to exploding, and whatever she did next would be so much worse than anything Valerie had suffered through yet.

Karen cleared her throat, drawing Valerie's unwilling attention.

"Will you do as I asked?"

"Yes." Valerie closed her eyes, the whisper of acknowledgment like a dagger to her heart.

Please, please let someone come for them soon.

It was a long shot of miracle proportions. But that was what they needed. A stroke of luck because Valerie understood that no matter what Karen promised, she'd eventually kill them all in her push to complete her research.

13

FERGUS USED A MAP and split the township, the lake, and the surrounding land into a grid. Tension and a sense of urgency slid through his gut. The letters contained little detail, but a thread of threat wove through every note.

His brother and his friend were in grave danger. He hadn't decided about Valerie yet, intending to reserve judgment.

Claire called out to him from the doorway. "I've come to join the search. I've closed the pub for two hours and will reopen this afternoon."

"No! It's too dangerous."

"I can't do nothing. Some of my regulars have volunteered to search the town and lake. There are twelve of us in total."

Fergus froze. "You didn't share details with the locals?"

Claire planted her hands on her hips and glowered at him. "That would be silly when this is a sensitive matter.

I merely told them you're concerned about your brother and his friend, and this absence is out of character. Fergus, they respect what you've done for the town and want to show their support."

But what if something happened to Claire? He'd never live with himself. Fergus wanted to protect her. He scrambled to think of a task to keep her out of danger and almost sighed with relief when he thought of one. "Actually, it would be a huge help if you could stay at the station and mark off the grid areas as the searchers report back."

"I could do that," Claire agreed. "It makes sense for you to join the search teams since you can fly."

"Thank you." Fergus scanned the group of humans—the locals—who intended to help in their search. The local fire brigade men had all turned up, along with several builders and members of the local rugby team. With this many people, they should search the entire town before nightfall. Gratitude filled him, relief that the locals would give up their precious free time to help find his brother and Finn. "I'll meet everyone outside in half an hour to divvy up our search areas."

"All right," Claire said. "I'll let everyone know and give them my contact number. Did you learn anything more from the papers we found?"

"The person who is blackmailing Valerie has her parents. I don't have a location, but it's in or near Te Anau."

Claire's brow furrowed as she stepped closer. "Do you know why or what Valerie is expected to do?"

"Whoever wrote the letters wanted Valerie to lure paranormal males. Other than that, I have no clue."

"Wait, do you still think the same person who tried to tempt your nephews is part of this?"

Fergus ran a hand through his hair. "Honestly, I have no idea. Maybe if we can find James, Finn, or Valerie, we might piece together what is happening. I don't know if Samuel's murder is related or something separate."

"Are you in danger?" Claire asked, moving closer to him, concern written clearly on her features.

A shudder ran through Fergus as memories of discovering Samuel in his garden emerged. "No one knew I was a dragon. My parents' arrival changed that."

"What did the man who spoke to your nephews look like?" Claire asked. "Maybe I've seen him around."

"The boys said he wore going out clothes, which we interpreted to mean a suit. He had long black hair tied back in a tail and a wrinkled face. He had a mole—the boys described it as a freckle—with hairs growing out of it. They also told us their wolves didn't like him, and he smelled like a predator."

Claire straightened fractionally. "That sounds like the man who entered the pub last week. He was strange but polite enough. He wanted to stay for two nights, but I only had a room for one night. I recommended he try the hotel on the lakefront. I don't know if he did or not because I haven't seen him since, or at least, he hasn't revisited the pub."

"Did he smell odd?"

Claire blinked, her surprise evident. "Smell?" She

thought back to the night in the pub. "I don't recall a distinctive scent. All I remember is the mole. It was hard not to stare."

"Was Valerie there? Did she recognize him?"

"Valerie served him. She didn't seem to know the man. He was...very demanding and exacting in his ordering. I served him the second time."

"Could Valerie have spoken to him later?"

"I don't think so, but it was right before she and the boys disappeared. He might've come into the pub while I'd popped out. Do you think he's dangerous?"

Fergus didn't hesitate. Given what he knew of Claire, she preferred honesty, and he'd give her as much as his job allowed. "If he's the one who murdered Samuel, then yes. If you see him again, don't confront him. Call me instead. All I want is to talk to him at this stage. He's a person of interest, not a suspect. Is it possible to get a copy of your security footage?"

"Yes, of course. I'll set it aside for you when I reopen later this afternoon," Claire said. "Wait, you mentioned you thought Valerie's parents were somewhere near the town? Why would they fly into the mountains if that's the case?"

"From the little I gleaned in the correspondence," Fergus said. "It would make more sense when you think about it. Hiding someone up in the mountains might be a way to keep others from finding the location, but there are practicalities like food and shelter to consider. Transport. If this person has Valerie, the boys, and Valerie's parents hidden away, and we've seen the man in town, they must be stashed somewhere close enough for him to drive. A property that's either rented or privately owned."

"That makes sense. That's why I own a pub, and you're the policeman. You think of these sneaky things."

Fergus went to her and drew her into his arms, giving her a quick hug before he pulled away. A familiar warmth spread through his chest, but he didn't act on it. Now wasn't the time. "I'll show you my map and the different grids."

More search volunteers arrived, and Fergus took the map outside. He pinned it on the wall and stood back, noting that his parents and Iain and Elspeth had joined the rear of their group. He dipped his head in silent acknowledgment before addressing the volunteers.

"First, thanks for coming to help. I'd suggest you pair up because we're uncertain what we're facing here. Ensure you have either the station phone number or Claire's cell number to report in once you've searched your grid or if you find something."

It didn't take long to assign everyone an area, and soon, only he, his family, and Claire remained.

"Iain, Elspeth, can you fly up to the hut and do another search of the area we checked the other day? Dad, I'd like you to fly over the properties on the edge of town in that direction." He pointed. "Work your way around the town and note any isolated buildings with vehicles parked nearby." He shrugged. "I'm not sure what to tell you to search for—anything that draws your attention."

His family wasted no time shifting and flying off to check their assigned search areas.

Fergus checked in with Claire. "Will you be okay?"

"No problem. How will I contact you if someone finds something?"

Excellent point. "I'll carry my phone in a pack. I'll hear the phone ringing and can land to contact you."

Fergus stole a quick kiss before he left. He jogged to his house and disrobed inside because he didn't want to distress the locals too much. They weren't used to him shifting at will, and he wanted to take it slowly. He grabbed a daypack, which would be easy enough to hold in his talons, as he flew and stuffed his phone inside before zipping the bag closed. Outside, he shifted rapidly, taking a few seconds to relish his stronger senses before he snared the pack and lifted into the air. As always, a sense of freedom and excitement filled him when he flapped his wings and became one with the air currents. The town spread out beneath him, the lake's sparkle coming into view.

Even as joy at the freedom of flight filled him, concern nagged at him. His gut told him they were on the right track with their search, but he worried about James and Finn. They might be young, but they were strong and intelligent. Neither was a pushover, and if what he suspected was true, for one person to hold them captive meant they'd been overwhelmed by force or surprised. Judging by the letters, Valerie hadn't been a willing participant, but how far would she go to save her parents?

Fergus flew across the lake, the water a deep blue color in the sunshine. The wind's resistance forced him to increase his wingbeats, but the flight to his part of the search grid took only fifteen minutes. A patchwork of trees and pasture spread beneath him, the ground undulating with hills and valleys cut by glaciers millions of years ago.

Although his instincts told him buildings were necessary to hold captives, he scanned every part of his area, even landing to search beneath tree copses or in gulleys. Any buildings, even the oldest sheds, had him slowing and using his dragon eyesight for intense scrutiny. It was obvious families lived and worked at the first and second farms. A farmer shifting a herd of cattle stopped to gawk at him. No, not the right buildings.

He continued flying, and it was at the third and last property that he thought he might've discovered what he was looking for. The place appeared deserted, yet a vehicle had driven along the track recently, the tire marks fresh after the rain they'd had last week.

Aware of possible witnesses, Fergus continued flying and returned to town after he completed his grid. Claire hadn't contacted him, but he'd like to hear from the other groups to learn if anyone had found places they should search more closely.

Fergus flew on the same trajectory as if he were merely out for a casual flight. He'd flown over this area before, but late at night when the rest of the town was sleeping. He couldn't remember seeing anything to raise his suspicions.

The flight back to town took longer than the outward journey since he fought with a strong wind that whistled over the mountaintops. But finally, he landed in his garden. He shifted and took two quick steps toward his kitchen door when he sensed someone behind him.

Fergus ducked to the right and glimpsed a hand holding a hypodermic needle.

His adrenaline surged, and he swept out his left leg. The person grunted. The hypodermic dropped to the ground. By the time he spun, his arms raised in a defensive position, the black-garbed figure was fleeing. They were familiar with his property because they sprinted straight for the gate and cleared it without pause. Fergus took precious seconds to shift and took to the air to hunt his quarry. Once airborne, he searched the vicinity, but the figure in black had disappeared. Several vehicles drove on nearby roads, and others were parked outside in driveways, but nothing stood out to him.

Fergus cursed inwardly and flew a tight circle of the town, gradually widening his search area. His assailant didn't reappear, and Fergus didn't know if he was hiding or had managed to reach a vehicle and escape that way. Maybe he shouldn't have taken the time to shift.

Sighing, Fergus flew back to his garden. This time, he surveyed his property closely before he landed again. He shifted and searched his garden. The hypodermic needle still lay where his assailant had dropped it. Fergus retreated to his home, hurriedly dressed, and grabbed a bag for the hypodermic. He'd take it to Nikau, who might help him determine what substance the man had attempted to inject into him. Fergus inhaled, testing the air, but to his frustration, he smelled nothing out of place. He needed Iain with his werewolf nose to help him.

He retrieved his phone and called Iain. There was no reply, so Fergus searched each room in his house. In his hurry, he'd left the door open, which meant the assailant might have entered his home. When he reached the room he used as his office, he immediately noticed the disturbed papers and his belongings in different places. Luckily, he'd kept all the information about Samuel's murder locked away in his office safe. He tried Iain again, and when he still didn't get a reply, he decided to check in with Claire at the police station.

Given the man who'd attacked him, should he walk or drive to the station?

Fergus pondered for seconds longer, then decided he'd walk with both eyes wide open. He'd check any vehicles he passed and keep his wits about him. At the last minute, he collected the bag containing the hypodermic and his keys. After checking he'd locked his windows, he secured his front and rear doors. The man might've jabbed him with the needle if his instincts hadn't kicked in. It was becoming evident to Fergus that whoever this man was, he *was* interested in paranormal creatures. But why?

Fergus's brisk steps took him down his driveway and along the road, but he slowed at each tree or bush and tried each vehicle door he passed to ensure they were locked. Any vehicle he found unlocked, he checked the interior and trunk. He didn't find anything incriminating during his walk to the station.

When he entered the station, he discovered most of the search teams were back already, their allocated areas much closer to town.

His parents, Elspeth and Iain, hadn't returned yet, and worry simmered in his gut. If any of them went missing, he'd never forgive himself.

"Any luck?" he asked Claire after making his way through the groups of chatting humans outside the police station.

"No," Claire said. "You?"

"I have one property I'd like to investigate. I returned to get backup before conducting a more thorough search."

"That makes sense," Claire said.

His parents arrived then, greeting several of the men loitering outside. Iain and Elspeth arrived not long afterward, and relief flooded Fergus.

"We have one possible property," Iain said.

"We didn't find anything interesting," Dougal said. "Although there is some beautiful land out there. I'm almost tempted to purchase acreage down here. It was the perfect day for flying."

Fergus smiled at his father's pleasure. His father was an optimist and saw good in everything and everybody.

"Iain, do you have a moment?" Fergus asked when his brother-in-law had finished describing the deserted property they'd flown over. Like him, they'd decided it was better not to land and search in case they got into trouble.

Iain followed Fergus outside.

"When I arrived back at my house, someone attacked me. They came at me with a hypodermic needle, but I got lucky. I sensed someone was behind me and moved the right way."

"Hell." Iain blinked rapidly, scanning Fergus from head to toe to reassure himself that he was okay. "Did you get a look at them?"

"Not really. They wore black and jumped the fence. Whoever it was—they were fast, and they'd disappeared by the time I shifted and flew after them."

"They jumped the fence?"

"Yeah, without hesitation," Fergus replied. "Can you come and do your tracking thing in my garden again? They were inside my house since some of my papers were disturbed. I want to know if it's the person we've been searching for around town. I couldn't smell anything out of the ordinary. You have a much better nose than me."

"Do you know what was in the needle?"

"Not yet. I'll get Nikau to look at it. Maybe he can shed some light on the mystery for me. I'll call him now and ask him if he has time to test it."

"What about the paranormal council in Auckland?" Iain asked.

Fergus paused. "I thought about them, but I'll see if Nikau can help first. The more information we have, the better it will be. We need to find this person."

"You didn't see their face at all?"

"No, it happened way too fast. All I know is they're fit, and they jumped the six-foot fence, clearing it by a good six inches. That, to me, screams paranormal."

"You call your vet, and then we'll check out your property to see if I can find the scent. I bet this is the person we've been tracking all over town."

"Possibly," Fergus said tersely, irritation crisping his tone. "Once I run the syringe over to Nikau, I'll assemble a team to help me search the two properties. Iain, I don't have a good feeling about this. I wish I understood what was happening."

Iain patted him on the back in silent commiseration, but it didn't help much. Instead, guilt ate at him. Had he and his family drawn the culprit to Te Anau?

14

"BE CAREFUL," CLAIRE SAID to Fergus. Worry had churned in her stomach since they'd begun their search today, and it refused to leave, no matter how much deep, slow breathing she tried.

After all the search groups had returned, she'd reopened the pub and told everyone to come for a drink and something to eat. This community spirit on display today required nurturing. Besides, the pub was large enough to hold them all while they discussed their next step.

"I will," he said. "But this is my job."

His expression softened, and wonder filled her. This time, the quiver in her belly held an entirely different meaning. She put her hands on his shoulders on impulse, stood on tiptoe, and brushed her lips against his. Fergus's swift intake of breath, the dilation of his pupils in the seconds before their lips touched, told her she'd made the right decision with this public display of affection. Fergus's arms tightened around her briefly before he loosened his grip and stepped away.

A wolf whistle came from his brother-in-law, and some of her customers hooted. Claire avoided their gazes, the heat in her cheeks instant. Not that she was ashamed.

She liked Fergus. A lot.

"Listen up, everyone," Fergus called, and the chatter faded to a pregnant silence. "We're dividing the search team into equal groups, one to check each site. Dad, Mum, and Elspeth will go with one group, and Iain and I will go with the other. We'll keep close contact with Claire, who will help us coordinate from the police station."

"I won't let you down," she murmured.

His grin was surprisingly sweet, and he drew her in for a quick hug before releasing her. "I know you won't. Does anyone have questions?"

"What happens if both searches are a bust?" the fire chief called.

"We'll have to widen the search area," Fergus replied. "Once we devise a plan, I'll ask for volunteers again."

Only Claire was close enough to feel the tension emanating from him. He was worried about his brother and friend and trying not to show it.

"George," he said to the fire chief, "can you take charge of your group? You know the area best."

Smart—giving the lead to the fire chief instead of one of his family. It put the men in that team at greater ease. It was fascinating watching Fergus at work.

"I want everyone to be cautious since this situation—from what we've pieced together—feels like a crime rather than a mere search and rescue. I want you to ensure you're never alone. If you need to split up, go in pairs."

These men respected him. Relief bloomed in Claire because she'd seen the graffiti around town. It was difficult not to, given the neon bright colors of the anti-paranormal sentiment. Fergus and his family didn't scare everyone, but some of the town's people were openly suspicious of Fergus now. It would take time for him to win them over, but she had every confidence that he would.

"Remember," Fergus said. "Keep in constant contact with Claire. Let her know if you hit snags or find anything." He paused, and his tight expression and clenched fist—the one nearest Claire—suggested he was struggling with something. After a long pause, he cleared his throat. "Approach the area cautiously because we think we're dealing with a paranormal creature. If we're right, they'll be dangerous, so if you find what we're looking for, I want you to back off. Observe only, and we'll regroup and come up with a workable plan. Any last questions?"

Claire's belly continued to churn while Fergus patiently answered questions from the men.

"We're uncertain about the specific paranormal creature we're dealing with. They're male with a lined face, a little taller than Claire, on the thin side, and they might have a distinctive mole on their chin. If you see this person, back off and contact Claire. She'll get the information to me."

Once men and women from the other group started to leave, Claire tugged at Fergus's arm. "Why do you think it's a paranormal? No one asked, yet that's a logical question.

The blackmailer could be a human with an agenda. Heck, it could be anything."

Fergus grimaced, gave a slight shake of his head. "It's a gut instinct."

Like she believed that. "*Fergus.*"

Fergus glanced left and right, took her by the arm, and marched toward the kitchen. She went willingly and ignored the catcalls from Fergus's sister. Once the door closed behind them, Fergus hugged her hard.

She stared at him when he loosened his grip, trying to read his expression. "What's wrong?"

"After I returned from my search, I landed at my police house. A man—at least, I assume it was male—tried to shove a needle into me. I fought them off, but they escaped."

Claire's throat constricted so much she could only stare at him, worry and unease ceaselessly knotting her gut. At this rate, she'd need to visit the pharmacy to purchase heartburn medicine. She swallowed hard, fear poised in her heart. "They—he tried to incapacitate you?"

"Yes. The common denominator is a paranormal status," Fergus said, his voice grim. "You should be safe enough, but I want you to take extra care. Keep aware of your surroundings and try not to be alone. Promise me."

Claire met his gaze, her expression solemn. "I promise."

Fergus hauled her close, hugging her tightly before kissing the stuffing out of her.

"Fergus!" Iain thumped on the kitchen door. "It's time to leave."

Fergus gave her another quick kiss. "Stay safe."

"You too," she said, but he was already striding for the main entrance with Iain. "Stay safe," she murmured. "Please stay safe and come back to me."

Fergus drove with Iain and three of the men from the volunteer fire brigade. He pulled up at the start of the dirt track that led off the main gravel road.

"We'll walk from here and use stealth," he told his group of eleven once they clustered together. "I'm certain this is the right place, but Iain will give us our answers. He's going to shift to wolf and go slightly ahead of us. If we see the man, I want you to treat him with extreme wariness. Iain and I suspect he's animal in origin because of his scent and agility, but it's possible he's a witch or wizard."

A couple of the men blinked while others shared looks, but no one commented. That was good. At least these men trusted him and Iain.

Iain stripped and shifted, not bothering a whit about his fascinated audience.

"Do you have to remove your clothes when you shift?" a fire brigade volunteer asked.

"Yeah." Fergus grinned. "Otherwise, the clothing bills become horrendous. My mother beat that lesson into us when we were kids. I'm sure Iain's parents did the same thing."

"Does it hurt shifting between forms?"

"A little," Fergus said. "But you become used to it, and the freedom of expanded senses and powers is exhilarating.

All right. We're ready. Watch your foot placement if we go into the trees because paranormals have excellent hearing. No talking. Try to communicate with hand gestures if possible. And finally, if the situation spirals out of control, retreat. There is no shame in backing off if it means saving lives. Report back to Claire if it gets to that stage. I want us all to go home in one piece and alive."

"Is this creature really that dangerous?" a man asked.

"Samuel was a werewolf. He was old but still in peak fitness. Someone murdered him. If we come across the man, let me and Iain handle him. We're unsure what he's capable of if he could take Samuel by surprise." And he'd tried the same thing with him. The man might've captured him if Fergus had been a fraction slower.

Fergus waited for comments. There were a few murmurs, but most of the men stood straighter, their features set in determination.

"Let's move out."

Fergus set a steady pace, following Iain, who trotted ahead. Now and then, Iain tested the air. They came to a bend in the track, still a fair distance from the property. Iain paused by a clump of gorse. He gave a low growl before backing up and shifting.

"What is it?" Fergus murmured.

"A scent-marking spot. I still don't know what the creature is, but they're animal if they're marking territory. It's instinctual for many shifters. We can't help our possessive nature," he explained to the clustered humans while Fergus texted Claire quickly that they were reasonably confident they had the right property.

One man, a retired cop and now a trekking guide, barked out a surprised laugh. "Does that mean we should be peeing on every corner in our gardens?"

Iain chuckled. "It would signal to a stranger the property is owned and valued."

The joking lightened the tension in their group. Iain shifted again, and they approached the property more carefully and maintained silence again.

Questions filled Fergus. Why did this man want to capture other paranormal creatures? Was he alone? He'd killed Samuel, which was odd if he'd taken Valerie's parents and was holding them along with Finn and James. He'd tried to grab him and lure away his nephews.

No matter how hard he pulled at the puzzle, Fergus struggled to find plausible answers. He'd come for Fergus prepared to jab him full of drugs, which meant he'd had a vehicle or a way of transporting him. The hypodermic needle signaled incapacitation rather than death. Fergus frowned. Maybe not. Hell, he felt as if he was blundering around and not seeing the right clues to help him find his younger brother.

His phone vibrated in his pocket, and he stopped to pull it out and check the message.

"The other group has cleared the property and is on their way here for backup. We won't wait for them. We'll keep going," he murmured.

The dirt track rose steeply to the crest of a hill. Although the men behind him tried to walk silently, their breathing was audible, and their boots scuffed the dirt as the incline took its toll. A bird squawked, and the man behind Fergus grunted at the call's unexpectedness. The treetops rustled in the breeze, and Fergus hoped it would be enough to cover the noticeable sounds.

At the top of the hill, Iain paused. He nudged Fergus's leg and indicated a long iron-clad barn to their right. Fergus signaled they were heading in that direction.

A fly buzzed, and he flapped it away from his face. It settled on his hand. Fergus stilled.

"Iain," he whispered. "This is the place. This is one of the purple flies." He lowered his hand, and the insect lifted into the air, buzzing away from them toward the buildings.

They had almost reached the entrance to the shed when a high-pitched scream of pain rent the air. Fergus froze, as did Iain and the rest of their group. The suffering in that sound raised the hairs at the back of his neck.

Fergus's instinct was to rush to the aid of this being, but he hardened his heart and sought precious moments to plan. He gestured everyone close and spoke in a low whisper. "I want four of you to go to the right. Walk around the shed and check for points of entry. I want the rest of you to come with me."

Another scream, different in tone but no less harrowing to listen to, resounded within the shed.

What the hell was happening in there?

15

"No, you'll kill them," a feminine voice cried.

Valerie.

Fergus recognized her voice. They were definitely in the right place.

Fergus tapped a rapid message to Claire. **Found them. Notify others to give us backup.**

Fergus put his phone away before signaling everyone to move. He pulled out his Taser and hoped it had enough juice to stop this man in his tracks.

When Fergus and Iain rounded the corner of the shed, the door lay wide open. Sunshine illuminated the interior and disclosed the full horror in one swift glance. Finn and James sat inside cages, their bodies slumped as if they were unconscious.

A pair of thin tigers in another cage eyed him, sadness and despair wafting off them. Fergus didn't know if they were shifters, but from their dejected air, they'd been contained for some time.

In another corner, a glass case contained too many of the purple flies for him to count. Well, that was one question answered. This guy was responsible for making the flies.

Fergus signaled his team. They crept toward the man who was focused on strapping a naked Valerie onto some sort of table.

The man stilled without warning and whirled. Long black hair framed a lined face. A distinct black mole marked the man's chin. For a long second, he and Fergus stared at each other. Rage contorted the man's face, his body. Damn, he was shifting. The buttons on the man's shirt gave way to reveal a bra.

As Fergus gaped, the man—no woman finished her shift and darted past with a speed that made Fergus blink. Her beast was something he'd never seen before—a combination of a dog and perhaps a cat. A long, skinny chestnut body with stripes across her flanks, and was that a pouch on her underbelly?

"Fergus! Shoot," a man shouted. Snapped from his shock, Fergus aimed and fired his Taser. He missed. Iain snarled and jumped the strange beast, but she flung him off, her frail and skinny appearance belying her strength.

Three of the men attempted to bar her way and lifted their guns.

"Stand down! Let her go." Fergus didn't want them injured on his watch. It was best if they let her escape at this stage. If she tried to remain in Te Anau, they'd make a plan and capture her.

The creature scurried out the door.

"Guard the perimeter and shout if you see anything out of the ordinary," Fergus called to the men. He plucked his phone from his pocket and called Claire. "Do you know where Mum and Dad are?" he asked the instant she answered.

"They're on their way to you," Claire replied.

"Are they in dragon form?"

"No, or at least they weren't when I talked to them. Have you found them?"

"Yes, talk to you later." Fergus hung up and called his mother. She and Nikau were probably the best bet for medical help. Fergus strode toward where Valerie was strapped to a gurney. Tears leaked from her blue eyes while dirt covered her cheeks. A long scratch down her arm looked infected, the wound red and angry.

"Shush," Fergus said in a gentle voice.

To his alarm, the flow of tears increased, and she sobbed. "I'm s-so s-sorry. This is all my fault."

"How?" Fergus asked, moving slowly as he unfastened the restraints. He kept his voice low and even so as not to distress her any further.

"Here," Iain said, appearing beside him in his human form. "Wrap this blanket around you to keep warm."

"Finn and James?" Fergus asked.

Iain placed a calming hand on Fergus's tense shoulder. "They're unconscious but breathing."

"What about the tigers?" He eyed the beasts. One hissed at him while the other remained still and silent.

Valerie wiped the back of her hand over her snotty nose. "Don't hurt them. They're my parents. I don't know what

Karen has done to them, but they've been in their tiger form since she locked us up here."

"We won't hurt them," Fergus said, although given their appearance, he wondered if the woman had damaged their minds.

"Fergus!" a voice roared.

His father. "In here, Dad," Fergus called back. To Valerie, he said, "You're a human."

She sniffed. "My real parents died when I was a baby. Jocelyn and Leonard promised my parents they'd raise me as their own, and they have, protecting me and treating me like the daughter they never had. I met Karen while I was working in a pub. I was desperate to remain independent, but my flatmate had run off the previous week with the rent money. My rent was due, and somehow, Karen got the entire story out of me and offered me a solution. At first, she only asked me to deliver packages."

"What was in the packages?"

"I don't know. I didn't ask, but I suspected drugs. One day after I visited my parents, she must've smelled their otherness on me. She'd been away for several weeks and arrived at my flat unexpectedly. She smiled and told me she had a special job for me and would tell me about it the following week. Something about her scared me half to death, and I was relieved when she instructed me to deliver a package. Then she left, and I didn't hear from her for two weeks."

"What happened next?" Fergus asked while watching his parents and Elspeth examine Finn and James. It looked as if they might be rousing.

"Karen phoned. She instructed me to integrate myself with you. When I refused, she told me she had my parents, and she emailed me a photo as proof. I thought she might've been lying, so I called my parents. When I didn't get a reply, I dropped by their house, and there were obvious signs of the struggle. The furniture had been knocked over, and some of the pieces bore huge gouges. Then, there was a terrible stink of what I think was urine."

"Marking territory," Iain said. "It was a sign. A thumbing of her nose at you."

"She'd tacked a note on the wall. It told me if I didn't follow her instructions, I'd never see my parents alive again."

"What did you do?" Fergus asked, wondering why the shifter had wanted him.

"I bought a plane ticket to Te Anau, then tried to work out how to get your attention. But after Claire gave me a job, Karen changed her mind and decided Finn and James would work better for her plans." She swallowed hard. "I didn't know what to do and felt I had no choice. I didn't want Finn and James in Karen's sphere, but she f-forced me to do her bidding. When James and Finn offered to take me on a flight, i-it was my chance to save my parents." She gulped and brushed away tears. "I didn't expect flying to be so scary and screamed. Finn tried to calm me, but I panicked. Not just because of flying over those mountains. Karen terrified me more. I don't know what happened after we landed near the apple orchard. Karen... I'm so sorry. Please, you must believe me."

"Shush," Iain murmured, cautiously patting her

shoulder.

"Why Finn and James?" Fergus asked.

"First, she'd staked out the residents of the town. She was severely pissed and raving about the old werewolf who refused to fall in with her plans."

"She killed Samuel," Fergus interrupted.

"Yes, she wanted him to help her capture you."

Fergus stared at her blankly. "Why did she want me?"

"She's a Tasmanian tiger shifter. The last left of her breed. She's also a scientist and was determined to increase the Tasmanian tiger population. When she was younger, she had a child. Settlers killed her husband and son. It did something to her and cracked her mind. From her ramblings, I've worked out she harvested her eggs and kept them while she tried to find a way to have live tiger babies. She thought my parents might be helpful since they're tigers, but the biology is too different. Next, she wanted to capture you and use your sperm to fertilize the eggs."

Fergus listened to the garbled details and tried not to feel sorry for this Karen. But her plan came from a disturbed mind. "She aimed for Finn and James when she couldn't get her hands on me."

"Correct," Valerie said.

"Why was she strapping you to the gurney?"

"Tasmanian tiger young inhabit a pouch, much like a kangaroo," Valerie said. "But Karen is too old to bear young. She intended to plant the fertilized egg in me, and once it grew to a feasible size, she'd remove the fetus and place it in her pouch."

"What sperm did she use to fertilize the egg?" Iain asked

194

in a hushed voice.

Valerie hiccupped and rubbed her nose. "I don't know. Either Finn or James. S-she had samples from both."

"Hell," Dougal said from behind them, shock vibrating in the exclamation. "This woman is a monster."

His father wasn't wrong. He'd seen some stuff in his time as a cop, but nothing that sank to these levels. His brother. Dragon fire! And Finn. The poor kid had suffered enough at the hands of his father from what Elspeth and Iain had told him. Neither kid deserved this crap. He wanted to tear after the woman, pick up her trail, and capture her so she couldn't repeat these atrocities. He tamped down his fury and his need for justice. *Focus, Fergus. Do this the right way. Think and plan.* "Dad, are Finn and James stable enough for us to move them?"

Dougal laid his hand on Fergus's shoulder. "That's what I came to tell you. I don't know what to do about the tigers, though. Every time we go near the cage, they hiss and snarl."

"They're scared," Valerie murmured. "I'll talk to them."

Fergus hesitated. "If you're willing to take responsibility for them, they can stay at the cottage behind my house. Samuel used to live there while he worked for me. I haven't had a chance to clean it yet."

"Thank you! I think that might work. We'll clean it for you. Thank you so much!" Valerie hastened over to the cage where the two tigers paced. They sniffed her and calmed noticeably when she put out her hand. The tigers took turns to nuzzle and lick her fingers.

His mother arrived and eyed the tigers with wary

195

suspicion. "Here are the keys. What will you do with the tigers? Can you trust them to behave sensibly? They're so thin. She must've held them captive for some time."

Fergus understood the subtext. The tigers might present a problem, but he could hardly turn them over to the authorities. Perhaps he could contact their clan leader. Yeah, that might work. "I'll speak with them," Fergus said. "Valerie is confident they'll settle. I told her they could stay in my cottage while they recuperate. Hopefully, this Karen Mercer hasn't damaged their minds too much. Look, they're responding to Valerie."

"Be careful, son," Dougal said. "From what the girl said, the mad woman has held them for weeks. We don't know what she did to them. It was obvious she cared little for their health."

Fergus squared his shoulders and met his father's wise gaze with a direct one of his own. "This is not their fault. I'll explain to them the consequences of injuring a human or another paranormal creature. With Valerie to reassure them, I think they'll gain confidence and become more trusting." At least, Fergus hoped that would happen. He didn't relish the idea of dealing with out-of-control tiger shifters. "Can I leave you to care for James and Finn? Get them back to Te Anau? Our local vet, Nikau, is the most likely source of medical help. He's a human, but his brother-in-law is a dragon. Claire knows where to find him."

"Will do, son," his father said.

"And make sure you watch for the woman. No one will be safe until we capture her," Fergus said.

"Goes without saying," his mother said.

With his parents and Elspeth overseeing Finn's and James's care, Fergus strode to the cage containing the two adult tigers. He fit the key into the lock and turned it but didn't open the door. "I'm Fergus Murray," he said. "The local policeman. Do you require medical attention? My mother and sister are both skilled in healing paranormal species."

"They're too weak to shift to their human form," Valerie said, tears in her eyes.

"That's fine," Fergus said. "You can ride in my vehicle, and I'll drop you off at my cottage. Feel free to use anything inside the pantry and let me know what you need in the way of medical supplies."

"I'll give you my number," Elspeth said from behind Fergus. "Valerie, call if you require medical help."

"You're being so nice," Valerie said, sobbing. "After everything I've done."

"You did it under duress," Elspeth said, speaking for Fergus.

"Fergus, give me your vehicle keys, and I'll run back and drive it to the barn," Iain offered.

Fergus dug in his pocket for his keys and handed them to Iain.

Iain did a half shift and took off at a sprint. Five minutes later, he returned with Fergus's vehicle, backing it into the shed as close to the tigers as possible.

Fergus hesitated, then spoke to his sister. "Elspeth, would you mind driving Valerie and her parents to my place? That way, you're there if Valerie requires help."

He jerked his chin in Valerie's direction, and Elspeth nodded, understanding his concerns without needing verbal interaction.

Another vehicle backed into the shed and stopped. The fire chief climbed out and strode over to Fergus.

"Can you drive my mother, James, and Finn back to their place?" Fergus asked the fire chief. "Take another man with you, so you're not alone on the return drive. I'll need your help once you're done."

The fire chief hurried off to help Fergus's parents while Iain stayed with Fergus.

"What should I do?" Iain asked, his attention on the case of flies.

"We need to photograph the entire area and collect every bit of equipment and any records she has left. Now that we have her name, we should obtain more information." He glanced at the flies. "I'll check with Nikau, but I'm not sure what to do with the insects. We can't let them loose."

"Agreed." Iain scowled. "Will you contact the paranormal council?"

"Yeah. I don't like it any more than you, but what if she starts up in another area? We can't allow that. We must stop her from torturing others in the same way."

"You're right, but the council people give me hives. I hated how they forced every paranormal being to register on their roll."

"I didn't like it, but you can see their point in a case like this."

"Having your name on a roll isn't a crime deterrent. I've heard stories about beings not registering."

Fergus released a heavy sigh. "Yeah, let's do our best here. We can debate later."

"Sorry," Iain said. "Would you like me to take photos? I'll work left to right and give the all-clear once I finish in each area. What the hell do we do with these flies for now?"

"Photos would be great. Let me think about the flies." He paused and wrinkled his nose at their incessant drone. Maybe another thing for the council to oversee. Yeah, that sounded like a plan. He'd make it clear how dangerous the insects were and give them photographic proof of the way they'd eaten into Samuel's leg. Decision made, Fergus gave instructions to the group of curious and milling humans clustered outside.

It was almost two in the morning when Fergus and Iain followed the last truckload of Karen Mercer's gear down the dirt track.

"Do you think she has left the area?" Iain asked as the lights of the Te Anau township grew brighter.

"I think she'll be lying low somewhere close because we have her equipment. I'm going to check with Nikau, but I think we have her supply of eggs and sperm in the portable freezer. If she's as driven as Valerie says, then she'll want those items back, at the very least, which is why I ordered the freezer packed in the back of my vehicle. We'll drive to Nikau's veterinarian surgery and ask his opinion."

"Smart idea to keep everything separated and on the down-low," Iain said with approval.

"My thoughts exactly. Karen Mercer is out there, and we'll need to watch for her. My gut says she'll strike and soon."

"Should we be worried about the family? The kids?"

"All the family, plus Valerie's family, are at greater risk. From today, we'll post guards. I'll ask for volunteers and station four guards at each property."

Iain nodded. "What about the vet's surgery?"

"I'm hoping we can sneak there, unload the freezer, and leave it with Nikau without anyone being the wiser."

"Why didn't you leave guards at the farm?"

"If Karen Mercer returns there, she'll be out of the way, giving us time to work out our next moves."

"And if she doesn't react in the way you think she will?" Iain asked.

Fergus shot Iain an enigmatic glance as he pulled his vehicle around the back of Nikau's surgery. "Then we're on our own. I've requested backup from Invercargill again, and my request was rejected when I mentioned paranormal. I'll contact the paranormal council as soon as I get home and take any help they offer."

Claire packed up at the police station and locked the building. Fergus had told her to take extra care because Karen Mercer was dangerous. He'd ordered her to lock her doors and not to go anywhere alone. He'd scared her, but once he'd described what they'd found in the deserted farm barn, her arguments had died a quick death. Poor Valerie. Finn and James had suffered, and she wondered how they'd cope after Karen's treatment. They'd been such cheerful and good-natured boys. Something like this would take its toll.

Claire had walked to the police station and hadn't realized how late it had become. The streetlights had switched on, and the dark shapes of vehicles, signs, and homes took on a creepy air. A frisson ran down her body, and she glanced over her shoulder. Nothing out of the ordinary. But her heart beat faster. She increased the length of her steps and broke into a jog, her nerves jangling.

The woman had been creepy in her man's disguise, and she'd hate to meet her in her true form. That she'd captured two tigers, a dragon, and a wolf without expending much effort made her extremely dangerous.

Claire turned the corner onto the street where her pub was, eager now to seek refuge indoors with her customers. She'd left one of her most reliable part-timers in charge, but he'd most likely need to go home to his family. Her steps slowed as she approached the pub because the front door was wide open. The building lay in darkness.

She screeched to a halt and pulled out her phone before retreating, her gaze never leaving the pub entrance. But before she could dial Fergus, a dark figure sprang at her, impossibly fast and challenging to avoid.

Claire tried to run, but the creature was on her before she'd taken half a step. She tripped, and her phone slammed on the ground. The distinct cracking of the glass face was the last sound Claire heard before her head collided with the pavement.

16

CLAIRE WOKE WITH A pounding in her skull and liquid trickling down her cheek. Confusion assailed her as she attempted to stretch her limbs. She couldn't move and couldn't figure out why.

"You're awake." The raspy voice wasn't familiar, not at first. Then Claire raised her head and met a woman's icy gaze.

The tiny hairs on her arms and legs lifted, and for a brief second, her breathing stalled before her heart slammed against her ribs. "What do you want with me?" She'd wanted to sound confident, but her words emerged in a scared whisper.

"Bait." The woman bared her teeth, her expression feral.

Claire recoiled, the wash of fear inside her growing into a storm. This woman wasn't right in the head. It was her eyes. They were dead, but the twist of her other features contained rage and savagery. She pushed her sneering face close, the hairs protruding from the mole on her chin brushing Claire's cheek. Claire lurched away, desperate to retreat. But she couldn't move. Numb. Her limbs must've gone to sleep. She flexed her arms. Struggled.

The woman laughed, a high-pitched sound that scraped along Claire's nerves. "Stupid girl. Luckily, brains are not required for you to complete your task."

Task? Claire inched away until she could go no farther. Thick bindings held her fast. Heck, she couldn't even crawl away from this scary woman if she wanted.

Sheer terror swept through Claire, her brain lurching from question to question. What the hell? Who was this woman? What did she want? What task?

The woman laughed again, but this time, she rose and put space between them.

Claire sucked in an unsteady breath. She tried to concentrate and corral her skittering thoughts. Yeah, she had to focus if she wanted to escape this crazy woman. She took stock, noticing the damp coolness on her back. A concrete floor. Bound. Smug woman.

The clues added together in a blinding rush, and she hated her conclusion.

This woman had captured and restrained her.

But why? Nothing made sense.

She recalled...

Claire frowned, prodding at her memories.

She remembered...

She remembered nothing! Her memories were a huge blank.

"Who are you? What do you want?" Claire demanded,

or at least she attempted to portray strength. That frightened little girl's whisper emerged again.

"You, my dear, are going to help me," the woman cooed. While her tone was soft, her eyes remained dead. She wrenched Claire's shoulder, pulling her upright and dragging her against the wall with effortless strength.

Claire thumped against the chill surface with force, the collision stealing the air from her lungs. She gasped hoarse drafts of air, her inhalations loud in the cavernous area. Water dripped in an annoying litany somewhere on the other side of the room. *Drip. Drip. Drip.* Like the thrumming of a countdown clock ticking toward finality.

Claire licked her lips when the woman said nothing further.

"W-what do you want me to do?"

Her obvious terror had the woman laughing again. The cackle sent tremors through Claire. This woman lacked sanity. There was something off about her. Something...

Claire tried to remember how and why she was there. How had this woman captured her? Who was she? And why did she want Claire? What did she expect her to do? So many questions, and she didn't have an inkling of an answer to any of them.

The woman cackled again, her pale eyes still empty of emotion. Claire averted her gaze and stared at her bound hands.

She wished she could remember something.

Anything.

Fergus dragged himself inside and flicked on the hall lights before going further. He scanned left and right and moved cautiously toward his kitchen after seeing or sensing no irregularities.

Clear.

He prayed Karen Mercer had left town, then he grunted, a harsh bite of the truth. She'd hang around and regroup. He'd wanted to track and keep up the pressure on her, but he was one cop. Another snort emerged. He'd heard from Invercargill. They didn't have the free manpower. Bastards. If there was one man he wished to let his dragon loose on, it was the area boss. Pompous ass. The Paranormal Council had been more helpful, although they couldn't send people immediately. They'd assured him they'd send two agents as soon as possible and had approved his action plan. One hurdle cleared.

His mother had assured him Finn and James would recover from their ordeal. Despite their severe dehydration, a meal and some rest would provide physical relief. Mentally—that was another story. He hadn't talked to his brother since Valerie had filled him in, but the formal interviews would occur tomorrow.

Valerie's parents were calmer now that they were with Valerie and had their own space.

He needed to learn from Valerie why Karen Mercer had chosen Te Anau as her base. There were still so many questions, and he found his investigation frustrating with limited backup. Ideally, he could have left officers to help his brother and the others while he and another team searched for Karen Mercer.

Letting her flee without chase galled him.

He sniffed the air, sifting through the various scents, and detected nothing out of place. At the barn, Karen Mercer's scent had been pungent—a combination of wet dog and wild game—which had struck him as peculiar. At other times, he had smelled nothing at places Karen had visited. The woman had a way of masking her scent.

Another question for Valerie.

Fergus searched the rest of his home, even peering under his bed in case someone lurked beneath.

Only then did some of the tension leave his shoulders. Fergus retraced his steps and opened his fridge to grab a beer. He stared at the contents, then decided he'd walk into the center of town and visit Claire. Maybe if she wasn't busy, she could share dinner with him. He might even find a dark corner and steal a kiss or two.

A glance at his watch told him it was almost seven. The pub would be busy, and he usually waited until at least eight before heading that way because of the evening rush. He opened the beer and dropped onto a chair at his kitchen table. The first sip was pure enjoyment, sliding down his parched throat. He took a second drink, letting his mind drift. Thanks to Valerie, they knew Karen Mercer was the last shifter of her kind, and she wanted to discover a way to create children of her blood using the eggs she'd saved. That wouldn't happen since they'd confiscated her equipment, including her last viable eggs.

"She wouldn't leave the area and all her hard work behind," Fergus murmured. "If I stood in her shoes, I'd..."

Fergus surged to his feet with such force the chair he'd

been sitting on flew back and hit the wall behind him. He grabbed his car keys and phone and was out the door before he completed the rest of the sentence.

If Fergus were in Karen Mercer's position, he'd strike back at his family or the people he cared for most.

Fergus jumped into his vehicle and called Iain.

"Hey, what's up?"

"No problems there?" Fergus asked, his chest tight as he waited for a reply.

"No, we're all fine," Iain said, sounding alert.

"What would you do if you were Karen Mercer and someone had stolen your life's work?"

"I'd strike back," Iain said without hesitation.

"Exactly," Fergus said, speeding down the street that led to the main road. When a hapless tourist attempting to park his campervan got in his way, Fergus blasted his siren, letting the din continue until the road cleared. He accelerated through the gap. His tires shrieked for purchase because he took the next corner too fast, but fear galvanized him.

The only other person he truly cared for was Claire.

"What is it?" Iain demanded, still on the line.

"I think Karen Mercer will go after Claire." Fergus roared around the bend, and the pub came into sight. The street and the pub were in complete darkness.

Fergus cursed.

"Fergus, tell me what is happening," Iain ordered.

"I'm at the pub. All the streetlights are out. The pub is dark. I can't see anyone."

"Do nothing until I arrive," Iain said. "You need backup,

and I'm the best you have."

Fergus didn't give Iain a hard time about his arrogance because his brother-in-law spoke the truth. Iain was the only one he could count on to have his back with Karen Mercer.

"Here, talk to your brother," Iain said.

"Fergus?" came Elspeth.

"Elspeth, I want you to listen closely. Stay indoors. Don't let the boys out of your sight until I speak to you again. Tell Mum, Dad, and the others to watch out for Karen Mercer." He paused, his voice breaking. "I think she might have Claire."

"I can help."

"No," Fergus said. "Stay with Mum and Dad. Watch over Finn, James, and the boys. Is Auntie still there?"

"Yes."

"Right. Promise me you'll stay together. Don't go anywhere alone. Promise."

"I promise," Elspeth said, obviously picking up on the note of panic in his voice. "But please call us and let us know what is happening. It doesn't matter how late it is. Call anyway."

"I will." Fergus hung up and surveyed the dark street. He hadn't received complaints or reports of the power being out in this area. In the distance, the streetlights glowed, lighting the streets and the shop windows. Only this street was affected.

A low growl—a familiar one—sounded from behind him, but Fergus still turned to check it was Iain.

"I arrived to find the street dark. I can't sense anyone

around, but I can smell Karen Mercer," Fergus said. "At least, I think I can."

Iain eased closer and sniffed the air. He gave a tiny growl and continued forward at a trot. Fergus followed him, the tension in his stomach increasing as they approached the open pub doors.

Like most beings with paranormal blood, he and Iain could see well in the dark, but their sense of smell gave them the most information.

Blood.

The coppery scent of it lingered in the air.

Panic unfurled in Fergus. Not Claire?

He swallowed hard and walked deeper into the darkness of the pub interior, letting his senses help him navigate the obstacles. Broken glass crunched under his boots, and he smelled spilled alcohol. Iain gave a low chuff of sound, and Fergus headed in that direction. A man lay on the floor in front of him.

Fergus stooped to take his pulse. "Still alive," he murmured to Iain.

He used the flashlight app on his phone to identify the human. A regular customer. Blood matted his hair. Someone had struck him over the head with an entire bottle of beer as a hoppy scent wafted from the man's clothes.

He called their local emergency medical team for help and the fire chief for backup. Then, he stepped in Iain's direction.

Another two men. He highlighted their faces in the torchlight and noted they were regulars, too. Both were still breathing and looked to have suffered the same fate as the first—a bottle to the head.

Where the hell was Claire, and why hadn't there been more customers?

They needed light.

Inspiration struck, and he called the power company to request aid. That done, he hustled after Iain. They discovered one woman and five more men, all unconscious. One man lay behind the bar, and Fergus recognized one of Claire's part-timers.

Fergus shone his torch and immediately noticed the smashed door. It led to the private quarters and Claire's office and was usually kept locked. Now, the wooden door hung drunkenly on its hinges. Fergus inched forward with caution. He kept catching whiffs of Karen Mercer, and his fear ratcheted sharply upward.

A rapid search upstairs produced nothing.

No Karen Mercer. No Claire.

Where was she?

Their last conversation had taken place at the old farm. He racked his brain. Where did they search next?

Iain morphed into a human. "Evidence suggests not much of a struggle."

"No," Fergus agreed. "This looks more like a tantrum."

"Yup," Iain said. "What next?"

"We'd better go back downstairs and wait for help to arrive. Once we have light and take care of the injured, we widen our search for Claire. We know she was at the police station. I told her to go home when I spoke with her almost three hours ago. She told me she intended to return to the pub and open as usual for dinner."

"The mess up here suggests that Claire didn't return."

"Yeah." Fergus led the way downstairs. The local doctor had just arrived armed with a torch. He blinked on coming face to face with a naked Iain.

His brother-in-law winked at the doctor. "The guy near the chilled beer seems the worst. They're all breathing, but the barman has a head wound. He copped the worst of the attack."

The doctor—a lanky man wearing glasses—blinked again but jumped into action. He darted behind the bar to crouch beside the barman, ordered Fergus to hold his torch, and ran gentle fingers over the wound on the man's head.

Two volunteer fire brigade men strode into the pub.

The doctor commandeered them and started issuing orders. "This man requires treatment at the surgery. Grab the stretcher from the rear of my vehicle."

The doctor approached the next patient, giving the woman a quick examination. "Unconscious. No obvious wounds. Damn, we need light here."

"I've called the power company. Hopefully, they'll have the situation under control soon." Recalling the woman coming at him with a syringe, Fergus said, "It's possible our fugitive jabbed her with a needle. I don't know the drug type, Doc, but Karen Mercer is a scientist. She could have injected these people with anything."

The lights blinked on without warning. They flickered off again before coming back and staying on.

Fergus spied a discarded syringe in the corner. "There's

the syringe, Doc. I'll bag it for you. Can you test its contents here?"

The doctor frowned. "We send our tests and specimens to Invercargill for analysis. We'll need to medivac these patients to Invercargill. I can't treat them all."

Fergus had expected this. "Right. Can I do anything else to help, Doc? If not, I have a fugitive to hunt."

Fergus's phone rang, and he pulled it out to check the screen. He didn't recognize the number, but that wasn't unusual. "Fergus Murray, Te Anau Police."

"I have your lady," a feminine voice rasped. "If you want her back alive, this is what you'll do."

17

FERGUS WENT COLD ALL over, immediately tossed back to that time when he'd learned about his best friend's murder. His fingers tightened on his phone as he listened to Karen Mercer's demands for her equipment and other property.

"You have two hours and not a second longer," she snarled.

"Let Claire go," Fergus said, his voice calm despite the panic, the out-of-control sensation roaring through him. It was like an echo chamber, reverberating with the helplessness he'd felt all those years earlier. "She hasn't done anything to you. She's an innocent human."

"Two hours," Karen repeated and disconnected the call.

"Crap." Fergus squeezed his eyes closed briefly before he opened them and took a deep breath.

"What does she want?" Iain asked, more likely to jolt Fergus back into cop mode rather than because he hadn't heard. Elspeth would've told him about Fergus's reasons for becoming a cop.

Fergus had been a child himself back then, but now he was an adult. He had training. He had backup. No way would this crazy shifter destroy the woman who'd wriggled under his skin. The woman he'd come to love.

"She wants the freezer with her eggs and the sperm. If we deliver that to the Lake Front Hotel, she'll give us Claire in return."

"Do you believe her?"

"No," Fergus said, every instinct telling him Mercer was a rabid, cornered dog. She'd do anything to prevail and to get her species to survive with her. Nothing else mattered to her. "The woman is unhinged. I think she'll kill Claire on a whim."

"Yeah, that's my reading," Iain said. "We need to bring in the family."

Fergus hesitated before nodding. "Not if it places them in danger."

"Fergus," the fire chief hailed him.

Fergus crossed the pub to join the chief. "Can you take point here for me? Karen Mercer has Claire, and she's threatening to kill her if I don't hand over the freezer."

"Hell." The fire chief met his gaze. "What are you going to do?"

"First, I need to clear the area around the Lake Front Hotel. This woman will use any person—woman, man, or child—she can get her hands on to further her cause. She is extremely dangerous."

"I'll use the phone tree to alert everyone. I'll help here

and ensure everyone gets away from the hotel area. How big an area are we evacuating?"

Fergus frowned. "To be on the safe side, at least three streets."

The fire chief stared, then nodded. "Right, you are. We'll have everyone meet at the school and tick off families as they arrive."

"Thank you," Fergus said, appreciating the man's calm acceptance. "If you need anything, call me."

"I'll ring if there is an emergency. Otherwise, we'll deal with it." The fire chief strode away to marshal his troops.

"Our plan?" Iain asked.

"We'll speak with Mum, Dad, and Elspeth and hopefully devise a rescue plan."

Claire sat quietly, not wanting to attract the woman's attention. The infamous kidnapper, Karen, she presumed. The woman was a nut job. That much was apparent in the way she paced and muttered under her breath. Sometimes in a foreign language Claire didn't recognize—not that her mind was working too well.

Her memories of the day were decidedly patchy. Karen even looked the part with her wiry hair sticking up in all directions. She halted and spun to glare at Claire.

"You think I won't kill you? Your man probably thinks that, but your people shot mine without compunction because we were different. I watched a farmer kill my mother and father and skin them for their pelts. The farmer left their bodies in a ditch and used their hides for seat covers. He came to regret his actions, as did his wife and four children."

Claire felt sympathy for the woman and understood her hate. It had been a different time, and humans were trying to change. The new laws were a start toward equality. Claire opened her mouth to offer her condolences but thought better of it and remained silent.

Karen didn't want an apology. She wanted blood, and if Claire said the wrong thing, it might speed up Karen's actions.

What man? Claire's recent memories didn't contain a man—not a particular one. This was most confusing. She knew her name and that she ran a pub. The events of the last days...no, weeks were murky. A few details scampered into her mind now and then. Loose bits of information that didn't seem to belong anywhere. Faces. Words.

She'd overheard Karen tell someone her plan. Her demands. A swap didn't seem likely because this woman had already admitted to murder. While the woman's grief was understandable, she shouldn't take it out on everyone she encountered.

"Then, there was my husband. We lived in Africa, and hunters shot him one day when he was on a run. With a high-powered rifle. He didn't stand a chance. I found him hours later. He'd hidden, but his wounds were too great for him to heal. I could do nothing but put him out of his misery. It was the worst day of my life."

Claire clenched her jaw to halt her appalled croak. She'd killed her husband. The man she'd supposedly loved.

Karen raised her chin and regarded her with scorn.

"What's wrong? You look as if you might vomit."

Claire didn't reply but merely swallowed hard.

"What? Nothing to say?" Karen mocked.

"What do you intend to do?" Claire asked.

"I'll get my freezer back with the contents—my eggs and the sperm I've collected—and I'll start over again." She cocked her head, her expression pure evil. "I thought I might kill you, but you'll be more use to me as a breeder. I'll stash you somewhere safe and retrieve you later. If I'm lucky, I'll be able to grab your policeman and perhaps the wolf. They seemed to be joined at the hip."

A breeder? Claire pushed at the heavy blockage in her mind, positive that she was missing a massive part of the puzzle. Please let this man have a plan to best this mad woman. *A breeder?* Did she mean to use Claire as some type of broodmare? Surely, this woman realized that any child she raised would be half something else. She'd seen the woman in her animal form, which meant she was one of these new paranormal creatures the government had made legal citizens with equal rights to humans.

Why did she remember this, yet she couldn't recall the events of earlier in the day or yesterday?

Could a human and a paranormal creature have offspring together? She frowned, her thoughts drifting. She'd always wanted to have children. Not that she intended to mention this to Karen. She didn't want to give the woman any reason to kill her now. Worry stirred in her belly, and she prodded at her memories, desperately trying to remember something more. Anything.

Karen resumed her pacing, her words no longer making sense, and Claire remained silent, attempting to come up with a plan. How did she escape this mess?

She'd witnessed the woman's speed and had no hope of running. Even if she could get free of the ties binding her. The woman had told the man she'd exchange Claire for this freezer, but she'd informed Claire she intended to keep her for breeding purposes. Given Karen's ranting, Claire doubted the woman's stability. Gut instinct told her she mightn't live through this exchange. She pushed out a soft sigh of resignation before her backbone straightened.

She didn't want to die.

The answers to every question remained murky, frustratingly out of her reach. She wanted to live, if only to learn the truth because every time Karen mentioned the cop, a faceless man entered her thoughts, and her heart fluttered. She softened. Sweet heat filled her cheeks, which meant this man was important to her.

If she could remember, the information might help to formulate a plan.

She started to ask questions before reconsidering her idea. No, best not to poke the beast. Instead, she'd take stock of her surroundings and try to reboot her memory. Meanwhile, she hoped the police were working to help her escape this jam.

18

"THAT IS THE SITUATION," Fergus said as he scanned the faces of his parents, sister, Iain, his brother, and Iain's brother, along with their visiting babysitter. Iain's boys were currently asleep while the rest of the family sat in the lounge, the sliding doors open to allow the evening breeze into the house. Beyond the darkness of the lake, Fergus spotted the lights of several properties. He stood, restless and needing movement to aid his thought process. "Niall and Connor will visit their cousins until we know it's safe for them here. That way, we can focus on capturing Karen Mercer."

"Done," Elspeth said. "I'll arrange it now." She turned to their aunt. "Can you fly them to Dunedin tonight?"

"The perfect opportunity to look up Matthew Dracon," his aunt purred. "He owns a chocolate factory there. I'm positive the boys would enjoy a tour."

"I'd love a tour," Iain said with a smack of his lips.

Fergus had learned his brother-in-law possessed a sweet tooth and had passed this on to his boys.

Iain glanced at Elspeth. "Once this is over, we'll collect the boys."

Elspeth grinned. "Done deal."

"Back to the situation at hand," Fergus said. "Does anyone have any suggestions about rescuing Claire and neutralizing Karen Mercer?"

"A beheading always works, no matter what the species," Dougal offered.

Iain shook his head. "She's fast. Really fast, and whoever tries that risks injury. The tiger is speedy enough to take care of her attacker and do fatal damage to Claire before we can react."

"Iain is right," Fergus said. "If we could get her out in the open, I'd suggest dragon fire, but this woman is smart. I doubt she'll fall for a scheme like that."

"The council?" his aunt asked.

"They're coming as soon as they can, but their resources are stretched thin. We can't count on them," Fergus said.

"What about those newfangled caffeine bullets that upset the clan leaders?" Fiona asked, her face serious and lacking her usual resident smile.

"I considered those, but you must apply for a license, which takes time. None of us has the proper qualifications or experience to apply. It's crunch time. We must get to Claire without putting her in jeopardy." Tension slid across his shoulders and sank into his gut. His hand trembled, and he squeezed his fingers into a tight fist to still the motion.

That madwoman had Claire.

His Claire.

He was a trained professional, but rational thought was damn tricky at present. He wouldn't rest easy until he held Claire in his arms. Fergus silently promised to spend more time with Claire and to kiss her often.

"What about silver bullets?" Dougal asked after a lengthy pause.

"But they don't work any longer," Fergus said. "Paranormal species have adapted to the point they can push silver out of their bodies."

"Think about it," Iain said, his security background evident. "You told us this Karen Mercer is a Tasmanian tiger—the last known one. As a scientist, she has kept to herself. She hasn't interacted with other paranormal species because word would've got around. She didn't register with the paranormal council because rumors would've reached us. Silver might still hurt her. At the very least, it might gain us enough time to get close enough to restrain her. Or hit her with a Taser designed to halt a paranormal being. Once she goes down, cuff her and collar her to keep her under control. From there, hand her off to the council and let them deal with her."

Fergus paced, analyzing his reasoning, nodding as Iain progressed. "That might work, and I have a weapon and silver bullets in my gun safe. It's old, but I inspected it recently and fired it at the test range. It worked perfectly."

"What if the silver bullets don't work?" Fiona asked. "Have you tried regular bullets? While she could heal herself, if we pumped enough into her, it might slow her reactions."

"Fergus, I think that's our best plan," Iain said.

"I can't think of a better one," Fergus agreed. "The only problem I see is if humans get in the way. While we cleared the area, some guests returned to their rooms."

Elspeth drummed her fingers on the arm of a chair. "She's chosen her place well because it means you can't place explosives or use fire or risk placing innocents in danger. That works for her, but how will she get away once she gets her demands? Does she have a vehicle? Have you checked the vicinity?"

Chagrin filled Fergus. "No, I've been too busy chasing my tail," he said. "She never mentioned the supply of a vehicle, which means she has a method of escape nearby."

"I hate to say it, but what's stopping her from killing Claire and then collecting the freezer? What does the exchange entail?" Fiona asked.

"She didn't give me a chance to ask. She listed her demands and hung up when I protested and requested further details." Fergus grabbed his phone off the charger and hit redial. He waited anxiously. Would Karen answer? Had she hurt Claire? That was his biggest fear.

"Where is my freezer?" Karen snarled.

The woman sounded unbalanced, and this disturbed him. She'd used his brother and Finn without hesitation, intent on her end goal. What was to stop her from doing something unexpected? He didn't, couldn't, trust her.

"We have your freezer and agree to your terms. We will place your belongings in the car park outside the main entrance of the Lake Front Hotel. In return, you will bring Claire, and we will do the trade face-to-face." To his relief, this emerged calmly and businesslike when he was anything but. The woman had his Claire.

"No, I'll leave the woman in my room."

"So you can kill her, and I get a body in exchange for your freezer. I don't think so," Fergus snapped. "Before I make the trade, I want to see Claire. I want proof of life."

Karen issued a delighted laugh that raised Fergus's hackles. Exactly what he'd been worried about. She didn't intend to return Claire. "I enjoy a worthy opponent. If you want your woman back safe, I'll take some of your sperm."

"I don't think so," Fergus said, working hard to keep his hostility at bay. "We agreed to a straight swap, and we're not changing the terms now."

"Keep your dragon and wolf friends away, cop. I can kill your woman and won't hesitate. Just give me my freezer, and I'll leave. No one gets hurt."

"Fine," Fergus said, even though he didn't believe her. The woman lacked emotions and didn't care who got hurt in her quest to breed Tasmanian tigers. "I'll be at the Lake Front Hotel in exactly one hour with your freezer."

"The contents better stay frozen," Karen Mercer said before he could hang up. "No deal if you haven't kept the contents viable."

"I'm not that much of a bastard," Fergus shot back. "Your samples have come to no harm at my hands." Which was more than he could say for Karen Mercer. She'd injured, kidnapped his brother, and killed others. "One hour. I'll be there."

Fergus disconnected the call. "Iain, you're a better shot

than me. She will come out with Claire, and if she has any sense, she'll keep Claire close. She'll be expecting us to try something."

"No, I don't think so. She comes across as arrogant," Fiona said. "Boys, you haven't commented. What are your suggestions?"

Finn swallowed hard. "She is egotistical and convinced her scheme has merit. Her way is right. The woman lacked empathy and laughed at us when we refused to do her bidding. She will use Claire as a weapon to bring you to heel. Nothing matters except her plan. It's her life goal, and she spent years developing the equipment necessary to achieve her vision. You've cornered her, and she's desperate. She's capable of anything."

"Finn is right," James said hoarsely, his eyes haunted. "She won't cease this madness until she's dead. Finn and I are better shots than Iain. Karen Mercer treated us like hunks of meat, and she raped us with her drugs and her bindings. We have to be there when you take her down. We can help," he said, his tone savage now. "I want to stop her from abusing other people and help to save Claire. Claire doesn't deserve this, and neither did we. This woman won't stop. You must make her."

Finn stepped forward until he stood shoulder-to-shoulder with his best friend. "We're helping you, and we'll be the ones to take her down. From memory, the silver bullets will fit several types of weapons. If we're both armed and shoot at her, at the very least, we'll distract her."

Fergus studied his brother and moved on to scrutinize

Finn. Despite their youth, they appeared remarkably mature in that instant. Fergus understood their need to help with Claire's rescue. He'd feel the same way if he stood in their shoes. Finally, he nodded.

"All right," he said. "This is what we'll do."

Fergus drove toward the Lake Front Hotel with Iain in the passenger seat. It was nearing midnight, and the streets were empty, with most people at home in their beds. One saving grace about this situation. "I hope this works."

"It will. The humans you've spoken to are ready. They know to shoot if they get a clear shot." Iain's phone beeped, and he checked the message. "Finn and James are in position. Elspeth says she, Dougal, and Fiona are in place on rooftops, prepared to use their fire."

"Good," Fergus said, regretting involving his family but having little choice. "I wish I could've kept the humans out of this plan, but I couldn't think of an alternative. We must shut this woman down, but…" Fergus trailed off, aware of potential complications. He'd attempted to explain to the fire chief and his men how dangerous this assignment would be. Each man told him they wanted to keep their family and town safe. They trusted him to guide them and wanted to do everything they could to help.

Their faith in him had been humbling, especially since this was a paranormal problem.

But so many things could go wrong.

It was the unknown components that had sweat coating

his spine and his hands gripping the steering wheel.

He parked his vehicle, pulled on the handbrake, and switched off the ignition. The resulting silence played on his taut nerves.

"Stop doubting yourself," Iain said, reading him with ease. "We've done everything we can to predict what she might do. Focus and trust in our plan."

"Do you think Karen Mercer will realize her freezer contents aren't original? I'm concerned the scent will clue her into our deception."

"Where is this doubt coming from?"

"Claire." Fergus screwed his eyes shut before opening them again and attempted to relax his tense muscles.

"You care for her."

"I tried not to, but she wriggled past my defenses. My paranormal status doesn't bother her, and she gets on with Mum and Dad."

"They like her," Iain said. "Elspeth does as well, and your sister is a tough nut. Once this is over, tell Claire how you feel. Spend more time with her."

Fergus swallowed. "I was trying to go slow. Miranda—"

"Miranda was a bitch, and when she left, we all cheered." Iain's response and his dislike were immediate. "She enjoyed playing with your head, and from what I saw, the entire relationship revolved around her desires."

Fergus sighed. "Not my favorite topic. It took me longer than it should've to understand my life was much easier when she wasn't around." He checked his watch. "We'd better go. Time to get this show on the road."

Claire kept her gaze trained on Karen. The woman was increasingly erratic, her breathing hoarse and audible. She muttered, alternatively angry, pleading, and tearful. Claire remained quiet, hoping not to attract the woman's attention. Her mood shifts and dead eyes scared the crap out of Claire.

Her memory still held blanks. Faces remained hazy. Her head thumped constantly, possibly because she was straining to reach those foggy friends and acquaintances.

Was there someone special in her life?

She didn't know, and her lack of knowledge sent fear spiraling through her. Instead of remaining immersed in her thoughts, she studied her dimly lit surroundings carefully, searching for a way out. She refused to give in or lose hope. The bindings around her ankles had become looser with her unobtrusive struggles for freedom. Unfortunately, the ones around her wrists remained stubbornly tight.

Few sounds pierced the building's walls. Had the police cleared the area, or was this a secluded place? The ground was cold beneath her body—concrete stained with oil. Perhaps a garage?

She'd heard Karen mention the Lake Front Hotel but couldn't recall if they had garages at the rear of their property. She'd visited once when the real estate agent showed her around the township's vacant businesses. One glance at the lakeside property had told her it wasn't for her, and she'd abbreviated her tour. Right after the hotel, the pub had immediately drawn her interest. Now, she wished she'd paid more attention.

Carefully, to avoid attracting Karen's attention, she eased her body around to survey the exits. Scant light pushed through dusty windows high on the walls. Just for natural illumination. No way through windows, then. Only one door, which limited her options.

"It's time," Karen said without warning. Claire froze like a trapped animal. Karen cocked her head. "I'll leave you here until they've brought my freezer."

"You're letting me go?"

"No." Karen's expression tightened, her mouth firming to a flat line. "I'll be back for you."

A cold threat tinged the woman's words, and a frisson of terror sped through Claire. Those dead eyes were so freaky. Karen didn't care if Claire lived or died. To her, they were all chess pieces in her way, and she would sacrifice those who no longer suited her purpose.

"Don't attract attention." Karen nailed her with a black glare. Her eyes shifted, turning a scary red before returning to standard brown. "Don't move. I'll be back once I've ascertained everything is going to plan." The woman stalked toward the door, and Claire watched. The added light from a streetlamp when Karen opened the door helped Claire to memorize the shed's interior. A jeep of some description sat on the far side, a large roller door in front of it.

The instant the door closed behind Karen, Claire pushed to her feet and managed to free one foot. Pain shot up her legs, but adrenaline had her shuffling across the concrete floor. Her gait was awkward, with her hands tied behind her, but she sensed Karen would kill her if things didn't go as she wanted. Any woman would work for her breeding plans.

Claire ducked into the vehicle's front seat and gaped at the keys dangling in the ignition. Although the vehicle's appearance was unimpressive, it could be her means of escape if it functioned.

A gun fired. Instantly, a volley of shots reverberated outside. Shouts filled the air. A feminine shriek of fury.

Claire hesitated, then ducked for cover as the door Karen had exited flew open, and she darted inside. She sprinted in the direction she'd left Claire and skidded to a halt. Her incensed scream caused chill bumps to prickle across Claire's arms, and she held her breath, trembling as she waited for certain discovery.

"Where are you, dragon's bitch? You can't escape me, so you might as well come out now."

Claire still didn't move. The roller door in front of the jeep rose without warning, and light flooded the shed.

"You're surrounded," a masculine voice called. "Come out."

The voice was familiar, but before Claire could fathom the speaker's identity, Karen released another one of her scary screams. Claire shuddered and scooted closer to the steering wheel. She wriggled her fingers, wincing at the pain. Her hands remained behind her back, but maybe if she positioned herself, she could turn the key. She had to try. With a careful twist, she turned her body and waggled her fingers again. God, they were so sweaty. She swallowed hard and managed on her third attempt to grasp the key.

"Where are you?" Karen screamed. "Don't make me sniff you out. Your punishment won't be pretty."

Claire's fingers trembled and slid across the key. She issued a tiny grunt of frustration. But on her fourth attempt, the key turned.

The jeep spluttered.

"Got you," Karen snarled.

Panic had Claire glancing over her shoulder. A mistake. *Ignore her. Hurry. You're wasting time.* She fumbled to release the brake and twisted her body so she could press the accelerator. The vehicle shot backward, colliding with something.

Karen released a horrific scream while Claire frantically tried to change gears with her minimal mobility. A shot cracked the air, then another.

Claire ducked as Karen screeched her fury. Seconds after another gunshot, a third scream held a gurgling quality. The gearbox crunched, and the jeep lurched forward. In gear. At last! But no, Karen had shoved the vehicle while trying to get to Claire.

"Claire, she's pinned by the jeep. Quick, get out and run outside." The order, spoken by a familiar voice, compelled her to comply.

She scrambled from the jeep, her exit inelegant and panicked. Claire glanced over her shoulder, tripping and falling. Karen's face looked wrong—contorted and animallike. The woman grunted as she shoved at the rear of the vehicle. It lurched forward, and she released a triumphant roar.

"Claire, move now!" the man shouted, panic reverberating in his words.

Karen was almost free.

Sheer panic had Claire scrambling across the concrete, struggling to gain her feet. Karen shrieked again, a hair-raising sound that pushed Claire to try harder. A man ran toward Claire and grabbed her, dragging her toward the door.

Karen heaved at the vehicle. She cursed Claire and the man holding her. The jeep jolted forward, and Karen flew at them, her hands growing wicked claws.

19

Fergus wrapped his arms around Claire and twisted their bodies to protect her. Sharp claws raked his back before the crack of a gun rang out. Karen shrieked, the sound full of agonized pain.

The gun fired again.

Bang. Bang. Bang.

Fergus rolled, taking him and Claire farther away from Karen. A glance showed blood covered the tiger shifter's shirt, and faint traces of smoke poured from a wound in her chest. *The silver bullets.* This part of their plan was working, even if nothing else was going right.

"Fire again!" he shouted, hoping Finn and James would hear.

Gunfire erupted immediately. His human volunteers were firing. Still, if it helped slow Karen down while he got Claire to safety, it didn't matter.

He shunted Claire to the right, but Karen kept coming,

the gunfire antagonizing her and affecting her temper. She ranted and raved, gesticulating and promising dire punishments.

"Give me back my property. It's mine. Mine!" she shrieked. Highly motivated and desperate, her strength seemed unstoppable.

Spasmodic gunfire kept coming.

Claire fought to stand, but her bound hands hampered her.

"Keep going," Fergus said urgently, pushing her on her way anyway because he wanted distance between them and Karen. "Roll," he ordered Claire. "Crawl as best you can."

He tried to keep low, giving Finn and James the best possible shot. Hell, talk about an ad-lib plan. They hadn't expected Karen to leave Claire in the shed, and once she'd done that, they had to decide if they should shoot straightaway or wait. One of his rescue team had an itchy trigger finger, and from the moment he shot, they'd had to scramble.

Karen sprang over him, her gaze on Claire. Claire glanced back, her face pale and her blue eyes full of terror. A gun fired. This one hit Karen on the shoulder. Either James or Finn had fired a silver bullet because she released a chilling scream. Fergus didn't hesitate. He flew to his feet and tackled Karen from behind. They went down in a heap, Karen grunting at the force of the impact.

She twisted and bucked beneath him, her wiry strength an easy match for him. She threw him off before twisting to grasp for Claire. A fireman had sneaked closer and was assisting Claire to her feet. Karen flew at them, and two shots rang out. Karen's dive continued, but the silver bullets had struck her. She crashed into the shed wall, even as her outstretched hands—claws—snatched for Claire. Her claws caught on Claire's jersey, but the human pulled her free. Another man came to their aid, and relief flooded Fergus once he realized Claire was out of harm's way.

"Fergus, stand back!" a voice shrieked. His sister.

He obeyed her order and not a moment too soon. Dragon fire rained down from above. Karen's wail had Fergus wincing. Her clothes and hair caught alight, but her caterwaul of defiance rang through the air. Finn and James stood behind him, weapons at the ready. Fergus edged away in case Karen tried to run at him or them in a last attack.

Not a second too soon. She leaped much farther than he'd imagined she could, springing at him with her claws outstretched. Flames flickered on her clothes. She didn't seem to notice, but heat seared his skin as she grappled with him.

Fergus pulled his dragon close to protect himself from the heat as he attempted to restrain her, but she yowled and roared, struggling with unexpected strength. Even this badly injured and covered with blood and smoldering clothes, she fought viciously with nothing to lose. Fergus grimly held on, trying to keep her from biting him with her protruding canines or scratching him with her wicked claws. He shoved her away, and she fell on her butt with a snarl.

"Duck," Finn shouted.

Fergus dropped and rolled, taking Karen by surprise.

Two seconds later, shots rang out, one after the other. Karen staggered. A third blasted her, and she went down, dropping to her knees. She groaned but crawled toward the freezer that sat out in the open. She left a sooty, bloody streak on the concrete behind her, and her plaintive keening would've broken the toughest man.

Fergus rose, not taking his gaze from the injured woman.

"What the hell does it take to kill this woman?" the fire chief asked, edging closer.

"Careful," Fergus warned as Karen clawed her way to her feet. "She is very strong."

"Last two bullets," Finn said, his voice holding the strain Fergus expected all of them were feeling.

"Fire," Fergus ordered.

Finn and James fired in unison. Karen twitched, and this time, a larger quantity of smoke pulsed from her chest, and she collapsed against the fridge. This time, she didn't move again.

Everyone fell silent. Iain strode over to join Fergus and the boys, still in his human form. "Is she dead?"

Fergus hoped so. "Cover me," he instructed, cautiously approaching Karen Mercer's still form. She didn't wince or make a sound when he touched her arm. He turned her over before crouching to feel for a pulse.

Unwanted sympathy poured through him despite the disillusions the woman had labored under. He couldn't imagine being the last of his race.

The lack of a pulse didn't reassure him. He had to make sure this woman wouldn't present a threat to his town or his family.

Fergus rechecked her pulse and poked the silver bullet wound. She didn't twitch, didn't make a sound. When he still couldn't find a pulse, some of his tension eased.

His father flew down from the roof and shifted, the dagger appearing in his hand. It flashed gold and ruby-red, even in the dim light.

"I can't believe you brought it with you on holiday," Fergus said.

Beside Fergus, Iain snorted. "That's what I told Dougal, but—"

"It's my responsibility to protect everyone from other paranormals," Dougal boomed. He stepped forward and prodded Karen Mercer with his toe. She didn't move. "We know nothing about her species. It might be best to sever her head. We don't want her to reanimate without warning."

Fergus shuddered inwardly. None of them wanted that, especially him.

"Thanks, Dad. I'd appreciate that, but perhaps we can wait until the humans have retreated?"

"We should explain the reasons and potential consequences. If you keep secrets from your human helpers, they might make mistakes later or assumptions that are dangerous to everyone."

Fergus considered his father's words. Given the lack of help from his colleagues in Invercargill, he needed his volunteers, especially for searches for missing trampers or other tourist-related calamities. This one-off case would never reoccur, but he should keep the volunteers informed. Fergus straightened. "You're right. I'll gather everyone together and explain what we're doing and the possible consequences if we don't."

He glanced around, searching for Claire. She stood between two burly volunteer firemen, and jealousy roared to life in him. He'd taken two steps before his brain kicked in. One fireman wrapped a blanket around her shoulders while the other cleaned blood off her face. They were old enough to be Claire's father, and their kindness to a victim did them credit. Neither deserved his jealous wrath.

He took a deep breath and crossed to her. "Claire, how are you doing?"

She frowned at him, her brow wrinkled. "Who are you?"

20

CLAIRE STARED AT THE big, sexy man standing in front of her. He wore a policeman's uniform, but she didn't recognize him. His features twisted briefly, and she thought she caught a hint of disappointment before his expression became enigmatic.

"Claire, I'm Fergus Murray, the local cop."

"We've called the doctor," the man on her right told the cop. "He's stuck at the clinic. Wanted to know if we could deliver her. We're getting a vehicle brought around, and one of us will drive her."

That made sense. He fought against drawing her into his arms and nodded agreement instead. It was a good plan. "All right. I'll contact the doctor later and ask about getting a statement from Claire. As for the rest of you, I'd like to speak to everyone, apart from whoever takes Claire. You can brief him later."

"Here's John now," one man said. "Don't you worry,

Claire. The doctor will fix you."

Claire felt strangely ambivalent about the entire situation. Maybe she was tired, or perhaps it was the jab Karen had administered to subdue her. Her stomach grumbled, and she decided it was hunger. Splotches of blood dotted the back of her hand, and she swallowed a whimper. She couldn't wait to have a shower. So tired. Her legs gave way, and she toppled, almost hitting the ground before the man who'd washed her face grabbed her arm. Her head slammed against his chest, and she saw stars, her entire world turning black.

"Claire!" Fergus turned back to speak with her before sending her off with John. He'd seen her waver but was too far away to catch her.

"Better get her to Doc right quick," Fred said. "Her breathing is normal, but I'm concerned about her blackout.

Fergus closed the distance between them, lifted her into his arms, and strode to the waiting vehicle. The young driver could easily carry Claire into the clinic, yet Fergus was reluctant to release her. She hadn't recognized him. He swallowed hard, not wanting these intense emotions swirling around inside him.

No time to dredge his memories or his feelings right now.

"John, tell the doctor she didn't recognize me, and she blacked out. Her breathing seems normal but suggest that he check for needle marks. It's possible the woman jabbed her with an unknown drug. She did to the others. They seem all right, but Doc should check."

"Will do," John said.

Fergus laid Claire on the rear seat, brushed her hair away from her face, and retreated to shut the door. He wanted to go with her, but with a sigh, he refocused on the tasks at hand.

"Gather around," he said to his volunteers. "I'd like to explain our next steps. I don't want any misunderstandings, so please ask questions, and we'll do our best to explain."

The humans gathered around him in a semi-circle near Karen Mercer's body. His father stood nearby with his dagger, and more than one human cast furtive glances Dougal's way. Fergus had to admit, his father was a scary figure when he wanted to be, and with his hair loose, his casual nudity, and the big-arse dagger, he was a sight.

"You already know Karen Mercer was a Tasmanian tiger shifter obsessed with breeding other shifters with her bloodline. She is what we call an old shifter. Werewolves, felines, dragons, and other species have evolved over the generations. Silver bullets used to be dangerous to many of us, but these days, we've become immune to the silver and can push it out of our bodies. Bullets containing a caffeine extract seem to work better to take down a shifter," Fergus explained.

"Does that mean you can't drink coffee?" the fire chief asked.

Iain chuckled at Fergus's side. "We drink coffee. The way I understand it is the process of manufacturing the bullets is different, and they combine the caffeine with other herbs. No one knows exactly what the company who invented them uses because it's proprietary information."

"In Karen's case," Fergus continued, "since she is an older being and had no offspring or fellow tiger shifters, we gambled she hadn't become immune to the silver."

"Why didn't we use the caffeine bullets, anyway?" a younger man asked.

"Simple," Fergus said. "Because no known paranormal beings live in Te Anau, they didn't supply bullets. The higher-ups decided we didn't need our allocation. I'll make the case for supplying every police station. Now, the next point: the silver bullets took Karen down, but some paranormal beings can regenerate. The best way to ensure they stay dead is to sever their head from their bodies and burn both parts of the body instead of burying them."

"Chop off their heads?" a muscular, dark-haired man asked.

"None of us want Karen to return to life and continue her plan. She had no compunction about abducting Valerie's parents and torturing them. Those of you who were at the secluded farm would've seen them. Her behavior toward Claire and the others was no different. Both humans and paranormals were merely tools used to further her plan."

Fergus watched the uneasy glances exchanged between the humans.

"What prevents this from happening to an innocent person?" the fire chief asked, voicing everyone's concern.

"Here, it's clear Karen Mercer was responsible because we have several witnesses, and we had to rescue Claire and the others from Karen's clutches. I believe in the law and have promised to uphold human law. As a dragon, I also adhere to the laws of my people. None of us take this step lightly, and we will offer traditional prayers for Karen's soul. Any of you are welcome to witness the ceremony," Fergus said. "I would like you to see that although she committed criminal acts, we will still treat her respectfully and behave within the realms of our country's laws."

"I agree with Fergus's proposal," one of the younger men said. "Even before we knew he was a dragon, he worked hard for our town and residents. Since we've learned of his dragon status, he has continued to act in the same honorable manner. With the paranormal reveal and new legislation, we must adapt to ensure fairness for all species."

"Adam is right," another young man said. "We should listen to Fergus and follow what he says. He is being upfront and explaining what he intends to do rather than treating us as ignorant humans."

Several of the men muttered agreement.

"Does anyone object?" Fergus asked because he wanted them to be unanimous in this decision. He, Iain, and his father would prioritize safety, but it would be better if everyone here bought into the plan.

"Do your ceremony," the fire chief said. "We will be your witnesses."

Fergus gestured to his father.

"Please form a circle around the body but stand well back. Give Fergus and me plenty of room. Sometimes magic spills from the dead shifter, searching for a new home before it disperses," Dougal boomed.

Fergus restrained his chuckle when the men hastily gave his father space. He removed his boots and clothing, placing them in a dry place before calling up his dragon. The nearby men gasped, but they made way for Fergus to join their circle.

Dougal recited several words in the old Celtic tongue, and Fergus felt magic sizzle in the surrounding air. The surprise on their faces revealed the humans felt the same power and awe as him.

When Dougal lifted the dagger, the rubies in the hilt shone brighter, and rays of vivid red brightened the scene. The glimmering silver blade seemed to thirst for the barbaric act. The blade's glow intensified, forcing Fergus to shield his eyes from the blinding light and heat.

When the heat faded, Fergus opened his eyes and turned toward his father. Fergus sucked in a deep breath and drew forth his fire. Flames shot from his maw, and he directed them toward the body, incinerating it with the force of his fire. An instant later, he cremated the head, and it was done.

The glow faded.

While Fergus shifted, his mother and Elspeth came forward to sweep up the ashes. He dressed and searched for the fire chief. He found the man with his volunteers, his face pale. Fergus crossed the distance between them with ground-eating steps. He'd hate this situation to trigger a fear of him.

"Is everything all right?" he asked.

The men faced him without the expected fear. Instead,

he saw awe and deep respect, which humbled him.

"No, nothing is wrong," the fire chief said, speaking for everyone. "The ceremony surprised us. We've never seen anything like it before. The woman got what she deserved for her actions. A trial through the courts wouldn't have worked." He studied Fergus. "Don't worry, you have our full support. You had it before we faced Karen Mercer this evening."

"Thank you," Fergus said, their trust humbling him again.

"We've discussed this, and we may face more situations like this. We might be a secluded town, but we see a lot of tourists. Or at least we used to before the pandemic. The numbers are increasing, but some businesses continue to struggle." He broke off and shook his head. "Sorry, I'm rambling. What I'm saying is that we stand behind you one hundred percent. As long as you're open and explain your plans, we're willing to continue helping you to keep our community safe."

Fergus managed a nod and thrust out his hand. The fire chief accepted his handshake without hesitation.

"Thank you," Fergus said, the sentiment heartfelt and shimmering in his voice. "Why don't you go home and spend time with your families? Have a hot meal and relax. You've all earned a rest." As the men turned away. "Please don't discuss this with others. The basics about the abduction are fine, but don't mention the ceremony."

"We won't," a younger man replied. "I doubt anyone would believe us, anyway."

Laughter erupted, and the humans exchanged grins

with Fergus and one another. The men raised their hands in farewell, and the group dispersed, leaving Fergus alone with the fire chief.

"Job well done," the man said to Fergus. "I and my men are here whenever you need us. I mean that. See you around, Fergus." The man clapped him across the shoulders and strode down the driveway.

Fergus watched the man until he disappeared before he joined his family.

"Everything all right, son?" his mother asked.

"Yeah. I'm pleasantly surprised by their acceptance."

"You'll have pushback from some in the town. It's human nature to give anything unusual the side eye," Elspeth said.

Fergus grunted. Wasn't that the truth? "What do you suggest we do with the ashes?"

"We're heading home," James said. "We'll help if you need us, but Finn and I are exhausted."

Concern wafted from Fergus's parents, and the same emotion radiated in him. He'd speak to his mother and ask her opinion, but his brother and Finn seemed subdued and might need the attention of a paranormal medic. "We'll see you at home then. Thanks for your help."

"We needed to see her die," Finn said in a hard voice.

"We did," James agreed. "See you later."

They watched the young men walk down the driveway with none of their usual impatience to get somewhere. Fergus scowled and turned back to his parents. "What's the plan?"

"We've kept the two piles separate," his father replied.

"Given the unknown aspects of her species, scatter the ashes in different areas. Send her head to the lake, her body to the high snow-capped mountains, and the residue of her potential offspring to the beech forests."

Fergus thought about the suggestion. "I agree. I'd rest easier if we did this straight away."

"Dougal and I will fly into the mountains," his mother said. "The ashes are ready for transport."

His parents transformed into their dragon forms, and his father scooped up the bag of ashes from Elspeth's upraised hands before they flew toward the mountains. Elspeth shifted, too, while Iain took possession of the second bag.

Seconds later, they took to the air, leaving Fergus alone.

Despite his strong desire to see Claire, this took precedence. He walked down the driveway to his vehicle. Earlier, he'd poured the contents of the flasks Karen Mercer had kept in the freezer into new receptacles. He hadn't replaced them in a freezer and had fought the guilt inside at consciously ending a species. Had Karen Mercer taken a different approach, the outcome might've changed.

Fergus placed the two bottles into a bag and undressed. He centered his mind and shifted. With the bag containing the bottles in his talons, he took to the air.

The beech forest surrounded the shores of Lake Te Anau, but instinct had Fergus wanting to fly farther from the town on the off chance that something went wrong. He didn't know what, but his gut told him to put more distance between his town and the flask contents. He beat his wings harder, slowly gaining altitude, and flew up the mountain and to the far shores of the lake. Once he could no longer see the township lights, he landed above the tree line. He removed one bottle from the bag and walked into the trees, purposely leaving the marked path he discovered and walking until he found a hollow tree. He opened the bottle and poured the contents inside the trunk, murmuring a farewell prayer in the dragon's old Celtic tongue.

That done, he retrieved his bag and flew over another mountain to a different forest at the edge of a smaller lake. He repeated the process, landing above the tree line. This time, he emptied the bottle into a crack in the limestone, repeating his prayer.

As he capped the bottle, which he intended to wash out in the lake before he returned to town, his prayer whispered around him. His parents. Elspeth and Iain. They had also recited the traditional prayer to send Karen Mercer to peace in the afterlife. Some of his angst and tension faded, and Fergus prayed the woman's soul rested easily now that the rite had returned her to nature.

21

When Fergus arrived at the doctor's surgery, he found his parents, Iain and Elspeth, waiting in the room set aside for patients.

"The doctor is still with her," his mother said.

Was that a bad sign? Fergus was unsure whether to panic. But eager to discover where their friendship might lead, he braced himself for obstacles. Fate was having a good chuckle at his expense.

The doctor emerged from a doorway to their right. He scanned their faces and smiled at Fergus, his manner calm and his eyes crinkling at the corners. "She's asking for you. Ten minutes. That's all. I've done bloods, and although I can't do extensive tests here, the basic ones tell me there is something foreign in her system. I've taken a sample and will send it to the lab at Invercargill. Mentally, she seems okay, although she has a lump on her head. I'm going to keep watch on her for the next three days. Physically, she has a broken rib and bruises and contusions. Her arm got banged up, and she's wearing a sling. All in all, I'd say she's lucky. Ten minutes and not a second longer. I want her to rest. Other visitors must wait until tomorrow to see her."

"Thanks, Doctor Howe." Fergus returned to his family and repeated what the doctor had said. "Go home. I'll drop by and update you after I've seen Claire. If you want, you can visit her tomorrow."

His father inclined his head and slipped an arm around his wife's waist as she began to protest. "Fiona, the boy is right. We don't want to overwhelm the girl when she feels ill. You tell Claire that I'll reopen the pub. Fiona and I will handle the damages and coordinate with the insurance representatives. I can sort out the staff and arrange cover for the bar. It will worry the girl. You tell her we'll look after the place."

"Thanks, Dad. I'll let you know her insurance company when I stop by. Mum, I'm starving," he added. "I don't suppose I can cadge dinner before I head home?"

Saying that was tactical because his mother loved to feed others. And distraction!

"I could do with food myself," Dougal said with a wink at Fergus. "We'll see you soon, son."

"Later," Iain said, nudging Elspeth from the room.

An instant later, Fergus was on his own and unaccountably nervous. He wiped his palms down his uniform pants and knocked on the door. The muted response, so unlike Claire's usual confidence, had him swallowing to moisten his dry mouth. It was his fault Karen had injured her. He shouldn't have told her to go home. In hindsight, he should've had her wait until he came to escort her home or arranged for someone else to drive her back to the pub. *You can't change anything now. Suck it up, buttercup.*

Fergus squared his shoulders and pushed open the door.

"Claire," he said, coming to a halt on seeing her pale, bruised face. One eye had swollen shut, and a snowy-white bandage wound around her head. A sling held her left arm in position.

"Fergus, thank you for coming to visit me."

"Why wouldn't I? Aren't we dating?" he asked, taking her knowing his name as a positive sign.

Her eyes and brows expressed surprise, but her face contorted in a frown halfway through. "We are?"

Fergus narrowed his eyes at her. "You didn't recognize me earlier. Did you hit your head? You know who I am now, or did you ask the doctor?"

"I struck my head more than once and have the lumps to prove it. I remember you now, but I didn't earlier. We're dating?" Her eyes were wide, or as wide as they could be, given her injuries.

"Is that worrying you?" Fergus forced out the words, not taking the gaze from her battered face. "We don't have to continue."

"I don't remember our first date," she said, avoiding answering his question.

"We went for a picnic. I flew you to a spot up in the mountains, and we ate sandwiches and drank a bottle of wine."

Her brow furrowed a fraction. "Ow!" She winced. "Did

we kiss?"

"Yes," Fergus said, and a blast of heat roared through him at the memory. "We've known each other for several months. We've done more than kiss."

"Oh. I don't remember. I'm sorry," she said, and her faint flush showed her discomfort at forgetting something this important. "The doctor told me my memories would return. I can recall things from six months ago, a year ago, but the recent occurrences are a bit more patchy." She stilled. "*Ohhh*."

Fergus grinned. "Yeah."

She paused and met his gaze. "Have we been dating long?"

Fergus hesitated before deciding to tell her the truth. "I was engaged before I came to Te Anau. Miranda lived with me, but she couldn't leave quickly enough after I confessed about my dragon status. We'd been engaged for a year before I accepted a job here. She preferred Auckland, and she ran back to her wealthy parents. Later, I heard she was engaged to a wealthy banker twenty years her senior. She had a big society wedding. That hasn't stopped her from calling and leaving messages about how unhappy she is in her marriage. But I'd met you and liked you a lot. Recently, I blocked her number and asked you out."

"Wow. Did I know any of that?"

"I shared some details to explain why I wanted to take our relationship slowly."

She cocked her head. "I'm getting the sense you've changed your mind about the slow part."

"Yes, but you not remembering me is a problem.

Miranda did a number on me. I admit it and fell hard for her. Until later, I didn't understand that her family never approved of me. That's why she never invited me to family occasions."

"Ouch. How could you not realize that?"

Fergus grimaced. "I worked a lot of overtime. It was during the riots and trouble when the anti-paranormal faction openly opposed the government's proposal to give paranormal species equal rights to humans. Only when I moved to Te Anau did her parents realize we were engaged. When I told Miranda I was a dragon, my confession didn't go well. She told me she was frightened I'd lose control when we were making love. She worried about what having half-breed children might mean, and most of all, she worried her family would cut off her trust fund. I tried to tell her we could live comfortably on my salary and she could get a job. That suggestion infuriated her."

"Definitely a bitch," Claire said, sounding more like her usual self.

"It takes two to argue," Fergus said. "I'm not perfect, but I was doing my best. Anyway, enough talking. The doc will come in and tell me I'm tiring you. Dad told me to tell you he'll take care of the pub."

"He doesn't need to do that. I'll be home soon."

"One arm out of commission will limit you." He traced a gentle finger over her bruised cheek. "Unfortunately, your face may scare away customers. Let Dad help. Honestly, he needs to keep busy, or he'll drive us all crazy. Karen did a bit of damage when she was trying to find you. Dad will handle the repairs if you tell me your insurance provider."

"I'll pay him," Claire said, her voice determined, even though she was fading and required rest.

"I'll tell you what," Fergus said. "You discuss the matter with him tomorrow. Mum and Dad will be in to visit you."

"I'm going home tomorrow."

The doctor stalked into the room. "Not true, missy. I'm monitoring you for at least three days. If you try to argue, I'll ship you off to Invercargill, and you can fight with the doctors and nurses at the hospital there. They're likely to keep you in for much longer and do myriad tests because of the paranormal involvement. They do like to stick their patients with big needles."

Claire gave a visible shudder.

The doctor's mouth twitched. "We'll discuss the matter tomorrow. I'd prefer to supervise you closely. The foreign substance the woman injected into your body could be anything. We don't know if you'll suffer side effects."

"Your insurance company?" Fergus prompted.

Claire told him, and he approached the bed. He bent over her and kissed a portion of her cheek that was bruise-free.

"Lips," Claire whispered.

"Are we continuing this dating thing?" Fergus countered. "Friends don't kiss on the lips." His voice emerged strained, and he didn't know what to do if she refused him.

"Yeah, we're dating," she said. "Now kiss me like you mean it, Fergus."

So Fergus kissed her and put every bit of emotion into

that kiss. Her lips were as soft as he remembered, and the lip lock must've gone on for some time because the doctor cleared his throat behind Fergus. His lips curved into a smile as he pulled away from Claire. He brushed a last kiss on her cheek before he departed.

"Later, sweetheart," he said. "Think about where we're going on our next date. Somewhere special since we're celebrating the fact we're alive."

"All right," Claire said, and although she looked exhausted, she radiated joy and happiness. "Can we fly?" Her eyes closed. "I enjoy flying with you."

"You remember." Satisfaction throbbed through him. "We can do anything you want," Fergus quickly assured, eager to bring joy to Claire. He had a great feeling about them. "Pay attention to the doctor and get well soon because I can't wait for our date."

Fergus exited the room with a spring in his step. Finally, his life was back on track, and Claire saw his true self. Honesty was a big part of a relationship, something he'd learned from Miranda. He shoved his ex out of his mind and strode from the doctor's surgery. His stomach gave a loud rumble, and he laughed aloud. His parents liked Claire a lot, and his mother would stop trying to fix him up with other women.

"Bring on our date," he said and started his vehicle, driving down the road toward his parents' rental. As soon as he got home, he'd call the liaison officer at the Paranormal Council, give a report, and remind them about picking up the flies.

He smiled, a slow satisfied smile of happiness.

His town was peaceful. A full moon hung above the lake, its reflection glinting in the dark waters. He opened his vehicle window and savored the scent of flowers from Mrs. Gregson's garden. A wolf's howl echoed from the nearby forest. Iain and his boys running under the full moon. He smiled as he pulled up outside the rental.

His family and the future beckoned. Fergus whistled a tune and hustled to the door, filled with positivity and a sense of ease. Despite a challenging week, he eagerly anticipated his date with Claire. Life—his life—was looking up.

Epilogue

Three Months Later

A cover band blasted an eighties rock ballad, and the crowd on the makeshift dance floor hooted and hollered. Claire grinned and continued pouring the order of four beers, a bourbon and coke, and a ready-mix gin.

The bell at the kitchen hatch rang, and one of her casual workers trotted over to grab the order and deliver it to the customer. Beside her, Elspeth and Valerie served customers. It was crazy busy, and fatigue clung like a second skin, but Claire loved the chaos.

"Did you see the dragons tonight?" a middle-aged woman with frizzy ginger hair asked, her words awe-tinged. "They're so big, so majestic, just amazing."

"They are a sight." Claire understood the woman's admiration. Riding a dragon was even better, but she wasn't about to share. She handed over the woman's drinks and accepted payment.

Business had picked up since word had spread about dragons and other paranormal folk living in Te Anau. It brought a few troublemakers, too, but Fergus and Iain soon sorted them out. Word had spread that the town's cop didn't stand for nonsense.

"Our local cop is a dragon," another woman replied while patiently waiting for service. "He's a lovely person. He looks after this town."

"I heard that," Frizzy Hair said. "Is he single?"

"No," Claire said firmly. "He has a steady girlfriend."

"Shame," Frizzy Hair said before leaving the bar.

Claire kept serving drinks, scanning the bar for potential problems between customers. A shout went up, and Dougal, Fiona, and Iain entered the bar.

"Hey, Dougal," Charlie, the local bank manager, shouted. "When did you arrive?"

"Flew in this evening," Dougal boomed.

"Yeah, we heard the commotion," another local said, his grin broad.

"We're taking a long weekend before we head back to the big smoke," Dougal said, referring, Claire knew, to Auckland and their farm to the north of the city.

Claire reached for the wine and poured Fiona a glass of her favorite sav blanc while Elspeth organized beers for Dougal and Iain. She leaned over the counter and kissed Iain.

"Where are the kids?" May, the owner of the local bakery, asked. She glanced around the busy pub as if she expected to see two juvenile wolves lurking amongst the sea of adults.

"We left them at home with our auntie," Elspeth said. "They're watching a Transformer movie. The ability to shift into cars fascinates them."

May laughed and melted into the crowd with her glass of wine.

"Where's Fergus?" Claire asked.

Dougal and Fiona exchanged a look, and when she glanced at Iain, he grinned and winked at Elspeth.

"He's busy right now," Iain said. "He'll be along later. It's a great crowd. Having music on Friday and Saturday nights was a fantastic idea."

"Elspeth's business brain at work. I can't wait for her gin."

"Claire's agreed to stock our gin," Elspeth broke in, her excitement palpable. "We're gonna do tastings starting next month."

Iain let out a whoop and snatched another kiss from his wife.

Dougal and Fiona beamed at Elspeth and extended their approval to Claire. They were such remarkable people. An extraordinary family. As always, her thoughts slid to Fergus, and a sense of love filled her.

The man—her man—was amazing, and she was crazy in love with him.

She thought he loved her in return, but he'd never given her the words.

And she ached for that commitment.

She was a lucky woman, but was she crazy to want more?

Dougal paid for their drinks, and he, Fiona, and Iain went off to find a table. Iain paused to speak with the band, which was between numbers. The lead singer grinned and nodded enthusiastically, and a customer waved for service, dragging Claire back to work.

She served drinks, took food orders, and chatted with customers. The happy atmosphere spread throughout the pub, and newcomers entered the local spirit. Shouts of greeting rang out, couples danced to the music, and the usual gossip abounded.

It took Claire a while to notice the gradual quieting of the celebrations, the hushed whispers, and nosy speculation. She cleared the bar and wiped it free of spills before Elspeth nudged her with a pointy elbow.

"What?" Claire asked.

Elspeth gestured at the doorway, and Claire froze.

Fergus stalked toward her, resplendent in his police uniform, his blue peaked cap that he didn't usually wear at a jaunty angle. His gaze was on her, his expression intent, and she wasn't the only woman who sighed.

Claire thought he'd stop at the bar, but she stared open-eyed as he vaulted over to land at her side.

Elspeth spat out a laugh. "Way to go, bro."

Fergus ignored everyone, his gaze still intent on hers. He closed the distance between them and kissed her—a sweet kiss that made her tingle to her toes.

Then, he pressed his forehead against hers. He rested there before he drew back a fraction and cupped her face in his big hands.

"I love you, Claire. So much. Will you please marry me?"

Heat and giddy lightness radiated through her. Her pulse raced, and a slow grin curled across her lips.

"Yes."

Fergus let out a whoop and lifted her into his arms. He strode from the bar, and the band burst into an old Joe Cocker song, the lyrics about up where she belonged and the crowd's cheers battling with her elation.

He loved her, just as she loved and adored him.

When they exited the pub, a shout rang out, and white petals fluttered around them, at them, and over them. Finn and James, enthusiastically aided by Niall, Connor, and their aunt, pelted them with petals.

Fergus paused, his strong arms flexing around her as he grinned down at her. "You said yes."

"I love you, Fergus. All of you. Your dragon. Your family. You, the man. I love you."

He groaned before he claimed her mouth, cementing their love and their future.

"Uncle Fergus. I have it," Niall shouted. "Auntie said it's practice for the wedding."

"Nah," James said, his eyes twinkling with mischief. "She told us Fergus must've been very nervous if he forgot the ring."

Claire barked out a laugh while Fergus rolled his eyes. He crouched beside Niall and Connor and accepted the ring box from them. Then he stood and opened the box, extracting a ring with a gold band.

"I love you so much, Claire Bryce." He pressed a gentle kiss to her mouth before pushing the ring onto her finger.

The red stone, with a black center, brought to mind an eye. The ring sparkled on her finger. Subtle engraving covered the band, and when she lifted her hand to look more closely, a dragon was etched into the gold.

"If you don't like the dragon eye stone, I can find something else in my hoard or make you a different ring—a more traditional one."

"You have a hoard?"

A faint flush filled his cheeks. "I'm a dragon. I collect things."

"Oh. Wait, you made this ring?"

"Yes."

Claire had thought her dragon couldn't surprise her much more, but it appeared she was wrong. "Fergus, I love this ring as much as I love you."

He beamed at her. "Can we get married soon? In Te Anau?"

"Yes," she said simply. "Whenever you like."

"Next weekend? A wedding on the lake?"

"Y-yes." She was so full of happiness it was difficult to speak.

Fergus let out a jubilant laugh, clasped her hand, and turned them to face the crowd pouring from the pub. "We're getting married!"

Congratulations rang out before Dougal hustled everyone inside and produced a box of champagne. He, Elspeth, and Iain poured and dispersed glasses of bubbles.

She squeezed Fergus's hand, and her handsome cop turned to her, the same emotions that bubbled inside her displayed on his face. He laughed and kissed her again. It was a celebration of love, and Claire had never been happier.

Thank you for reading **Hunted Pack.** You might've already guessed that I adore dragon-shifter romances. If you do, too, you'll be pleased to know that I have more available dragon romances. Check out my Dragon Isles series today. (https://shelleymunro.com/dragon-isles/)

ABOUT SHELLEY

USA Today bestselling author Shelley Munro lives in Auckland, the City of Sails, with her husband and a cheeky Jack Russell/mystery breed dog.

Typical New Zealanders, Shelley and her husband left home for their big OE soon after they married (translation of New Zealand speak - big overseas experience). A twelve-month-long adventure lengthened to six years of roaming the world. Enduring memories include being almost sat on by a mountain gorilla in Rwanda, lazing on white sandy beaches in India, whale watching in Alaska, searching for leprechauns in Ireland, and dealing with ghosts in an English pub.

While travel is still a big attraction, these days Shelley is most likely found in front of her computer following another love - that of writing stories of contemporary and paranormal romance and adventure. Other interests include watching rugby (strictly for research purposes), cycling, playing croquet and the ukelele, and curling up with an enjoyable book.

Visit Shelley at her Website
https://shelleymunro.com

Join Shelley's Newsletter
https://shelleymunro.com/newsletter

ALSO BY SHELLEY

Troubled Mates
Broken Pack
Cursed Pack
Hunted Pack

Dragon Isles
Liza
Cherry
Rena
Sasha

www.ingramcontent.com/pod-product-compliance
Lightning Source LLC
Chambersburg PA
CBHW031342020726
47499CB00005B/1366